THE FIELDS WE FLED TO

Aria J. Turner

For Poppy, whose fate was to read my books in the clouds.
For those who laughed at me for getting rejection letters.
For Mom and Dad. I finally finished one.
To Breanne, you push me to be the best writer and friend I can be.

For all those who are still wounded from war and have scars that are more than just skin deep.

CONTENTS

CHAPTER 1

September 8th, 1940, 1:30am, London, England.
James

Sirens.

Loud sirens.

Huh, that was odd.

Wait, sirens?

My eyes snapped open.

Bloody hell.

Sirens.

Bomb sirens.

I threw off the blankets I had been wrapped up in and leapt from the rickety wrought iron bed. The only other thing in the dull room was a dresser and a suitcase to the right of the bed.

Without thinking, I grabbed the suitcase. We'd done drills before, so many times I could do this with my eyes closed.

But this wasn't a drill. We didn't receive a broadcast.

This was real.

It was actually happening.

"Mum?" I called as I raced out of the room.

"I'm downstairs, James," my mum's voice yelled back at me.

I hurried down each step, trying to flick strands of golden hair out of my face. It was a mess. I couldn't see where I was going half the way down.

My mum was waiting for me at the bottom of the stairs in her nightgown and bathrobe. My father was close behind her, wearing almost the same pajamas as me: a matching set of loose pants and a button up shirt.

"Come on, James, quickly," Mum said to me before I took the lead, hurrying out the back door.

As I crossed the threshold and ran out onto the lawn, the ground shook a little, and the sirens grew louder, sending a ringing through my ears. It was dark, too dark to see where my feet were hitting the grass. The street lights would have lit up the night, but they weren't supposed to be on for fear it would show Hitler where to drop the bombs.

That didn't seem to matter now.

The only saving grace was the lights that flickered in the distance, illuminating the sky in an orange glow, and even that insignificant observation wasn't without consequences. It was coming from downtown London, and they weren't street lights.

I reached the cellar at the end of the yard, the wood on it still new and unblemished. We'd just built it a month ago as the city's fear of an air raid grew.

Sadly, that fear had now become a reality, and it was quite possible that we would get blown to bits.

My hand flew to the steel handle that had been bolted in place and violently opened up the large hole in the ground. I jumped in with my suitcase Mum and Dad not far behind me.

Dad closed and locked the door from the inside, engulfing us in darkness. I rummaged around for a flashlight, and almost gave up before I felt my hand touch a metal cylinder.

Found it.

I flipped the switch, and the room was bathed in an eerie glow. Soft yellow light bounced off the walls until Mum reached for the large hanging lightbulb and pulled the chain.

It filled the dark space with golden rays, but it would short out for a second, flickering before coming back to life.

The room shook.

It was large enough for all three of us to stand up in, but I didn't want to. I knew there were spiders lurking in the support beams, and as much as I didn't want to say it, they bloody scared me.

The cellar had two large benches on either side of it with thin mattresses placed on top of them, accompanied by mismatched blankets that we found hidden in a corner of our attic. At the very back of the bunker were shelves containing books, a few decks of cards, and any canned food we could get our hands on.

The shelves at stores were barren as people were preparing for the worst. It seemed as if we were going to be locked in here forever.

I hoped to God that wouldn't be the case.

The lightbulb's chain wobbled a little every time the walls quaked. I watched the light go back and forth and started to feel dizzy, my stomach doing flip-flops.

We sat in silence for a long time, as if speaking would alert the Germans to our location. That was, until Mum looked at me.

I knew what she was thinking.

I needed to get out of the city.

Many younger children had been fleeing, going into less populated areas of England and staying at relatives' houses. Mum had talked about it a lot. She had asked my uncle if I could stay with him if something like this ever happened and he had said yes.

"Tomorrow," she said, in a tone that meant it wasn't up for discussion.

"Tomorrow," I told myself, but in a hushed voice, afraid the Germans had somehow found a way to hear us down here.

The room shook again, and I clenched my fists so tight my knuckles started turning white.

That was, if we managed to survive the night.

September 24th, 1943, 11:43pm, Naples, Italy
Mara

I was running.

I was running faster than I probably should've been.

My brown hair would have been tightly pulled into pin curls if I wasn't running this fast, but now, the locks were a knotted mess.

I heard voices around me, coming from the streets surrounding the alleyway.

Fretta, Mara, fretta.

Hurry, Mara, hurry.

This wasn't supposed to be happening.

This *really* wasn't supposed to be happening.

I felt my heart racing, matching how my mind felt.

They couldn't catch me. Not with what I had hidden under my maroon dress.

I'd be dead.

Just another corpse in the Germans' wake.

They shouldn't be here.

This was our country.

They didn't belong here.

The things that were under my dress burned into my skin like a branding iron.

But I knew they weren't. I knew it was just my imagination.

Sweat started to form at my hairline and I felt a drop trickle down my forehead. *Napoli's* humidity was bearing down on me mercilessly, leaving me a damp mess as soon as I stepped outside. Even though it was *mezzanotte*, it was still *dannatamente caldo.*

Too damn hot.

I heard footsteps an alley over and ran faster, failing to slow my breathing. I tried to make my lace-up leather heels click softer on the uneven cobblestones. It was difficult to watch out for the divots in the ground where my heel could get caught and twist my ankle.

I'd done that a few times.

And because I couldn't help being loud, I just kept picking up speed.

"*L'hai sentito?*"

Did you hear that?

Merda.

"*Si.*"

Another voice.

I pressed on, turning into another alleyway.

Just a little farther. Just a little farther.

My legs felt weak having run about a kilometer through back alleys.

It wasn't easy.

Queste accidenti scarpe.

These damn shoes.

I was going to have blisters.

If my feet weren't already bleeding from the non-conforming leather.

They were new. I would've never worn them in the first place, but according to Luca, they were supposed to help me blend in.

Because a Southern village girl could never fit in in a big city such as *Napoli*.

I'd also never worn cropped pants under a dress either, but they had pockets and pouches to hold the various items of contraband in my possession.

It was hard to run with the things stuffed into my pockets, and I was afraid that the contents were going to spill out at any moment.

I wondered where Luca and Amelia were. They had gone in with me. We separated though so it was easier to get away from the soldiers who not only had this corner of the city on lockdown but who were also looking for local thieves.

I turned another corner, and that was when the alleys became familiar. I slowed my run to a light jog. I was so close.

Luca should have already been there, he was the first to start running.

Amelia was coming from the other side of the street, though, and that was a different set of alleys. Ones she'd mapped in her head in order to prepare for the escape.

She knew those alleys like the back of her hand. She'd lived in this part of *Napoli* for as long as she'd been alive.

Me, not so much.

I had to walk them five times before I could remember which twists and turns to take, and which alleys ended in dead ends.

I took a deep breath and poked my head out, peering left and right onto the street.

No soldiers.

I made my way out of the alleyway, turning right.

I made it.

The safe house of *la Resistenza* loomed in front of me.

I let out a breath of air and hurried up the steps.

My hand outstretched and opened the door, which was always unlocked unless someone had decided otherwise, and stepped inside.

On the outside, the safe house looked like a wreck. The steps that led up to it were cracking and weathered down to almost nothing. The railing on the side that had helped many *nonne* make it up the stairs wasn't going to be much help anymore. It was crooked and rusted as if someone's touch could reduce it to a pile of dust. The cobbling of the walls was cracking everywhere, and the paint had been peeling.

The inside, however, was beautifully wallpapered, with whimsical furniture and light fixtures. It was meant for people to feel comfortable.

The outside was for people to look at, and keep walking.

I let out a sigh of relief before turning to go into the front parlor.

Amelia should be coming in soon.

And that's when I heard it.

"Per favore non farlo!"

Please don't.

I recognized the voice.

It was Amelia's.

And I recognized the voices that came after it.

Harsh.

Deep.

Northern Italian.

And then the same harsh, deep, voice but in a language I didn't understand.

Merda.

No, no, no.

I should've run outside and put a stop to what I knew was happening.

I should've.

But I couldn't. I'd be caught too.

If I came out with a gun in my hand, I'd jeopardize my part of the mission. We had the lot of us go in for a reason. We knew there was a chance one of us could fail.

So I just stood away from the window and prayed to God that she found some kind of heaven.

Madre di Dio, proteggila.

Mother of God, protect her.

BANG!

I heard a muffled scream, something fell, and all of a sudden, there was a ringing in my ears, and it wouldn't stop.

My hands started to shake, my breath hitched in my throat.

I did nothing to stop Amelia from getting shot.

My heart rate started to accelerate as I began to pace the front parlor, wringing my hands out, trying to keep them from moving. It wasn't working.

The things that I'd stolen from the supply truck were burning my skin, seemingly through the cloth of the pants.

I had to take them out.

I disposed of two pistols, several rounds of bullets, and a couple of hand grenades, along with a box of gunpowder, throwing them down on the coffee table.

Amelia had been carrying the heavier stuff because

she knew the area so she could get around faster. But if she was noticed, well, it was kind of hard to walk past a woman carrying two machine guns on her shoulders.

The pistols gleamed at me, as if winking. My labored breathing continued, and my heart quickened its pace ten-fold.

I *couldn't* slow my breathing. I tried to count to five over and over again but it wouldn't stop. I switched to counting to twenty, but it still didn't work.

I knew something was off. It'd happened before. It was what others called a panic attack.

Whatever that meant.

I had to sit down, my legs felt like they were going to give out. I fell onto a lounge chair upholstered with green fabric, but I still couldn't stop myself from shaking and felt my foot start bobbing up and down. The sound of the gunshot kept replaying in my head, Amelia's last words playing fast, then slow, and then I heard the body drop again and again.

I raised a shaky hand to my mouth trying to muffle my heavy breathing as if the soldiers who had just killed Amelia would hear it through the walls and come into the house, kick down the door, and shoot me in this chair.

The ringing in my ears got louder, and I found myself bending over, putting my head between my legs, attempting to block everything out.

1, 2, 3, 4, 5, 6, 7, 8, 9...

It wasn't working.

In the distance, I heard footsteps coming from inside the house, but it was like I was hearing them through glass.

"Che c'e, Mara?" A voice flooded my head.

What's wrong?

I opened my mouth to speak, but no words came out, just another loud, shaky breath. I felt a hand come to rest on my shoulder, and someone's hand slowly lifted my head up.

"Mara?"

Luca.

He was here.

He tried to calm me down by rubbing my arm, telling me everything was alright.

But it wasn't alright.

Amelia just got shot.

Yet, after a while, I started to believe his words.

Slowly, my heart rate started to go back to normal, my hands stopped their tremors, and the ringing in my ears got quieter.

My breath was still shaky though. It wasn't going to be easy to get it back to normal. It would probably stay that way for a few more hours.

But I was fine.

Luca was fine.

Everything was fine.

———————

"You want to what?" I yelled, my voice carrying across the dining room of the safe house.

This was not okay.

Filomena's dark eyes bore into mine. There were other small groups like us around *Napoli* and scattered across the north. Our group was small, but not too small, and she happened to be the leader.

A leader who had just really pissed me off.

"*La Resistenza* has been talking about getting our younger members out, and I think recent events have proven that we can't lose more of you. A war zone is no place for our children."

The room was silent. There were ten of us. There would've been eleven, but-

That wasn't important.

We couldn't look back.

The people of resistance never looked back.

"But-" I tried to get out before Filomena's piercing dark eyes stopped me.

"All resistance members under eighteen have been assigned safe houses."

Sixteen, seventeen, eighteen...

Two years.

Damn it.

"A select group of good Samaritans have agreed to open their homes far away from here. We've been given ours."

"Where?" Luca asked, finally deciding to join the conversation.

Filomena's gaze flickered over to him and she sighed, "*Inghilterra*."

"*Merda*," Luca and I both breathed out, glancing at each other.

Inghilterra?

As in... England?

As in... English-speaking England?

Merda.

"How are we going to get there?" I asked, preparing myself for any kind of plan.

There were only two of us who were under eighteen: Luca and I.

And I was glad it was just the two of us.

I didn't think I could trust anyone else.

"We have a man in the city who's willing to forget the

color of his uniform to help the children of this country."

I raised an eyebrow, "We're being escorted by an ENR soldier?"

Esercito Nationale Rupubblicano.

The National Republican Army.

Mussolini's henchmen.

The people who had betrayed our country by supporting him.

Filomena nodded.

"This is a set up," I breathed.

"No, it's not. The soldier has a personal stake in it, he won't rat us out."

I scoffed, "Like what? He cares for the children of *Italia*? To that *cazzo*, we aren't the children of his country," I snapped.

Filomena gave me the look that she had reserved just for me.

Shut up.

That's what it meant.

Shut up, you're just a child.

I ignored it, "Seriously, Filomena, what personal stake has he lied about having?"

She let out a sigh. It must have been tiring, me always being this way: defiant, slow to trust, seeing every flaw in every plan we'd ever made.

But she couldn't get mad at me for it, it was what made me such a good asset to *la Resistenza*.

"*Tu, Mara.*"

You.

Me?

"*Aspetta, cosa?*" I said, blinking.

Wait, what?

"He says he wants to make sure you're safe."

"*Chi e lui?*"

Who is he?

"Someone named Marco."

My face fell.

That *cazzo*.

"What a load of *cazzate*," I mumbled, inaudible to anyone other than Luca, who let out a muffled huff in agreement.

Marco.

The coward.

He was the epitome of a traitor.

When a person decides to join the military when they turn eighteen instead of joining the Resistance with their girlfriend, there's something wrong.

Marco did that.

And I would never forgive him for choosing that horrible man over what we had talked about fighting for since we were old enough to get involved in politics.

About freeing our country from the fascist rule of the dictator.

But instead, when I turned 16, and left our small town in *Abruzzo* to help fight for what was right, he was already halfway to *Roma* to apply for the ENR.

He broke my heart.

Not because he didn't join me, but because he had sworn to fight for the very thing that damaged our rights as people.

That was evident as soon as German forces started inching their way into *Italia*.

"Is something wrong, Mara?" Filomena asked me, but it didn't seem like I should respond that yes, actually, something was terribly wrong.

"No. Sorry," I muttered.

She lifted her head a little higher and looked to the rest of the group, "I'm pleased with what we were able to accomplish in previous weeks. The next few days are going to be hard, and the battle to come will be difficult to win, but we will fight. Luca, Mara, you can go upstairs and start packing up. You depart in the morning."

I was about to open my mouth to protest, but Filomena shot me a look, and I bit my tongue.

I was a lead strategist, and I was good with a gun. She needed me here.

But no, she didn't. She needed me twenty-five thousand kilometers away because I wasn't an adult yet, and I couldn't handle what was going to happen in just a few days. Though I was old enough to endure everything before it.

Luca nudged me, "*Andiamo.*"

Let's go.

I nodded, Filomena watching my every move as I made my way out of the dining room.

I was *incazzata.*

It was bad enough being shipped off like little kids, but Marco escorting us made it humiliating.

As soon as we were out of earshot of Filomena and the rest of our group, I let out a groan, climbing up the stairs to the second floor of the safe house, where most of us slept.

"I can't believe they're sending us away."

Luca shrugged, "I can't believe they didn't do it sooner."

"They need us here."

"No, they don't. They have enough support in *Napoli.*" He paused for a second, knowing I didn't believe his words, "They'll be fine without us, Mara."

I scoffed, "We started this. *We* need to end it."

"Mara, be glad they don't want to openly send a bunch of kids into a war zone like *i Nazisti*."

I shivered a little thinking about the things I'd heard when we weren't supposed to be listening to the meetings in the dining room. Ten-year-olds who were given rifles and told to fight for Hitler in a war they couldn't possibly understand.

I was almost seventeen, and I wasn't even sure I understood.

When we got up to our room, Luca opened the door for me. I nodded my thanks and walked into the small room.

There were two tiny beds on either side of the room, thin blankets draped across them. The ceiling slanted to each side, forming a point in the middle and both them and the walls were covered in flowered emerald wallpaper. A small wooden nightstand sat in between the rickety beds and a window was situated above the nightstand, letting moonlight stream into the dark room.

The floor creaked as I walked over to the lightbulb hanging from the ceiling. I tugged on the string, which illuminated the room with a low golden glow. We walked to our respective beds, and as I crouched down to get a small leather suitcase from under mine, I glanced back at Luca.

"I'd just rather be fighting here than sitting on my ass over there," I groaned as I pulled the suitcase out.

Luca laughed, "You just really don't want to be dragged there by your ex."

"Hey, we never actually, you know..." I trailed off.

He nodded, understanding what I was trying to say.

It wasn't an option to talk to someone who was on the other side of a war. So, there was an unsaid separation that had occurred as soon as he decided to leave for *Roma*.

I heard from his brother, Gino, that he had done it.

Gino was killed five days later in a raid performed by the ENR.

And Marco didn't give a *merda*.

I opened the suitcase and made sure I had everything in it, reaching back under the bed for the few spare shirts and skirts I had misplaced.

There was no closet, so everything that Luca and I had was stuffed into the suitcases we had, or put under our pillows.

I only had one thing under my pillow.

And it was the only thing I cared to remember to take with me.

I grabbed the pillow, and reached in until my fingers brushed against metal, and I wrapped my hand around the grip, pulling the gun out. A Beretta pistol, fully loaded, and two extra magazines. It was my father's before the Fascists took over the Italian government. That was before the people loyal to the Democratic Italy were silenced by Mussolini and his growing power.

"What do you think England will be like?" Luca asked, packing his own bag.

His voice snapped me out of my trance, making me stuff the gun and ammunition into a hidden space behind the fabric at the bottom of my suitcase. Luca's side of the room was a lot more disorganized, and his clothes were thrown everywhere. They ranged from under the bed, to laying on it, to stuffed under the mattress.

"I don't know, never been."

"Yeah, you and me both."

I huffed, "This is going to suck, Luca. We're going to be sitting around in some little town where we don't know anyone, and where we're going to be expected to relax, and pretend everything's fine. I don't think I can do that."

"Well at least you know English," he muttered.

Merda.

Before this war started, and we were still in school, I was fascinated by the English language. I loved how it sounded, so much more static than the melodic sound of Italian, and so I had become obsessed with learning every word I could.

I knew a lot more than I probably should have.

For an Italian, our language was our pride. We didn't learn others' languages, they learned ours.

"I know how to say 'hello' and 'how are you?' but after that, I have no idea what I'm doing," Luca said with a smile.

He hated anything related to school, he couldn't be bothered with learning a different language.

"My English isn't that good," I said, trying to downplay what I actually knew.

"Says the girl who read Mary Poppins in English," Luca mumbled.

I wanted to change the subject. I hated the fact that I knew English. I was always asked, "Isn't Italian enough for you?" In *Abruzzo* if a person spoke English, you were stuck up and a *stranzatta.*

A bitch.

So I kept my mouth shut.

The rest of the town only thought I was learning a few phrases, Luca was the only one who knew I could speak almost fluently.

We told each other everything since we were three.

Our parents were friends.

There was no getting rid of him.

I had tried.

Mailmen don't take boxes without stamps with a 1st grader's handwriting scrawled on the top saying *New York, America.*

I really did try.

"What do *you* think England's going to be like?" I asked.

Luca laid down on his bed, all his stuff crammed into his suitcase, sticking out the sides after the thing had been shut and pushed off the mattress.

I sat down on my own bed, the thing was hard as a rock but it was all *la Resistenza* could spare, we had too many people and no money.

He looked up at the ceiling, "*Bella. Molto Bella.* I'm excited to see the farms, and the fields, and the cows, and all the green."

I laughed a little, "We have all of that here."

"I know, but I want to see it there. And *Londra*, I want to see *Londra.*"

"*Londra* is blown to bits, Luca."

His face fell, "Well, when everything's back to normal, and when the Allies win the war, I want to see *Londra.*"

I looked at the cracked floorboards, "I don't think things will ever go back to normal, Luca, even if the Allies do manage to win."

"They have to," Luca breathed out, his whispers almost incoherent.

My hazel eyes flickered back over to him, and managed a sad smile, "It's good to hope, *fratello.*"

Brother.

I didn't have any siblings, but Luca was as close to a brother as I was going to get.

We were family under the Italian flag, and we were family under the belief of freedom for our country.

That was family enough in a time where family was

uncertain.

I latched my suitcase up, hoping all the clothes and shoes in it wouldn't make it pop open.

"We should probably get some sleep," I said, peering at the rusting alarm clock next to my bed, "We only have a couple hours before Filomena comes knocking on the door telling us to get our asses up."

Luca nodded as I slowly placed my suitcase on the floor before going over to the light, turning it off, and plopping back down on my bed.

My eyes looked up at the flowered wallpaper for a second as I let my head fall to the pillow. They fluttered open and closed, before I slowly started to give into slee-

"Mara?"

I groaned to signal to Luca that I was still, barely, up, "*Che cosa*?"

What?

"Do you think the Allies will win?"

I wanted to lie, I really did. I wanted to put him at ease. To tell him everything was going to be fine. To give him hope.

But I couldn't.

"There are times when the good guys don't win, *fratello*," I paused, letting out a breath, "Let's pray this isn't one of them."

CHAPTER 2

September 27th, 1943, 2:20pm, Plymouth Station, Plymouth, England

Mara

Silence.

That's what could describe our trek to get here. Three days of travel. Sometimes hidden and sometimes not, in almost complete silence.

When we left, Marco and I had been civil to each other, curt nods, the occasional forced smile. We had known each other for most of our lives, we weren't going to ignore each other outright.

Our mothers taught us better than that.

Though when he offered to help me into the car that drove us across Northern Italy into France, I had sharply refused.

I could take care of myself. I didn't need him helping me.

And other than the informative 'keep walking,' 'keep your head down,' and 'turn left here,' we hadn't spoken. Not even when we were crammed into the back of a farmer's truck, covered in hay, having to scrunch up close together to make room for the three of us.

When we made it to Spain, partially by walking, he needed help undoing his uniform. Spain was neutral in the war, but they had Allied sympathies, so showing up in the ENR's uniform wasn't the best way to make a first impression. I had helped him, but didn't look at what I would have if I wasn't helping undress a traitor.

We'd slept in fields for the entire journey, and our first night, we didn't even sleep.

That was the one thing that Marco and I had in common, we had soldiers' mindsets. We would keep going, even if that meant not sleeping. We could go without sleep, and still be fine, because that was what we'd been trained to do.

Luca and I hadn't changed clothes. I was still wearing a thick navy straight skirt, along with a shirt jacket made out of the same material, with a nice collar and large pockets on either side. Brass buttons held the thing together, and the jacket ended at my hips. I had also changed out of the uncomfortable shoes that were given to me with the purpose of blending into *Napoli's* northern fashion, and instead, wore my favorite leather boots that were laced together by leather cords.

My hair was pulled into a ponytail except for two bunches to the side of my face that were pinned in swirls to keep out of my eyes. My hair was in waves, something that people had told me in Italy was a blessing. It wasn't. I found it easier to do my hair when it was standing flat as straw instead of stubborn and wavy.

Once we made it to Spain, we kept going, all the way to the farthest northern point, which Marco had said was Santander. From there, we purchased ferry tickets to get us to England. Very few people were on that boat.

I wouldn't want to be going there if I was in Spain.

In Spain, people didn't get blown up.

We were just moving from one war torn country to another.

Now, I was standing in the center of Plymouth Station and I felt like I couldn't breathe in the crowds. Businessmen in dark suits raced past me, while young people with suitcases stood around, still trying to flee to the country.

I was holding my suitcase in one hand, and my ticket in another. Marco had passed it to me as soon as we crossed into English waters.

We stood on the platform, just Marco and I. Luca had gone to purchase a newspaper, something about how he wanted to look like a local.

I looked straight ahead. I wasn't interested in talking to a traitor.

A train passed by with a screech of its brakes. I checked to see if it was ours after it came to a stop, which sadly, it wasn't.

The loud sounds of the horn whistled to signal it was leaving.

"I love train stations," Marco said, trying to break the uncomfortable silence.

"*Si, anch'io.*"

Yes, me too.

"Mara, I-"

"No, Marco."

"But we need to talk."

My gaze snapped over to him, my hazel eyes locked with his green ones. His hair was lighter than mine, almost matching the olive color of our skin.

"Marco, there's nothing to talk about, you swore allegiance to the very people who took away our freedom. Who took away our *lives*. You betrayed your country. You betrayed *me*. I think that covers it, don't you?"

Our eyes were locked. He wasn't going to budge and I wasn't going to be the one who looked away either, as if I was daring him to break eye contact.

He didn't.

"Mara, I'm sorry, I-"

I couldn't help myself from scoffing a little, "No apology in the world could ever make me forgive what you did."

"Mara-"

"You hurt me, Marco," I hissed, trying hard not to raise my voice in the train station. I was speaking a different language. In this war, that was dangerous. "You broke my heart. You left me. You left your country, you left your *famiglia*. You left us for the people who want to kill everyone in their way. You know me better than anyone, you know I don't shatter like a little porcelain vase. I might crack, but I don't shatter. But what you did, *that* made me shatter."

I felt a hand close around my own and I couldn't help let my eyes close for a second. For a moment I let my skin remember how it felt to have him hold my hand, how they seemed to fit perfectly, how they'd been calloused from farm work.

I looked at him.

"Mara, *ti amo*, you know that. And that never changed. When I went to *Roma* I thought about you every day, every night, even when I got placed in *Napoli*. I thought about you when I heard of the growing *Resistenza* in the area. So when word got around to some of us who were less loyal to Mussolini that they were trying to sneak kids out of Italy, and Filomina told me about getting you and Luca out, I couldn't say no. I wanted to protect you."

"If you thought about me so much, and wanted to protect me so much, then why do you wear the uniform of a regime that has sworn to destroy people like me?" I said, pulling my hand away from his. I couldn't do it.

I couldn't keep remembering all those good times that we had.

Those stolen moments at midnight, when we'd sneak out of our houses and meet in his family's vineyard.

The days we'd spend at school passing each other notes about our future with each other.

Those times at the beach where we talked about having a house with a vineyard and olive orchard. We'd sell our own *vino* and *olio d'oliva.* We'd have two kids who could tell each other everything, and would be two pains in the ass, but we'd love them anyway. I'd be in the Royal Army, while he stayed home with the kids.

We'd argued about that one quite a lot.

Those memories, they had to go away.

Because they reminded me of how much I missed him, how much I missed *us.*

He left you, he turned his back on his country, and he takes orders from a man who is insane.

Marco pursed his lips, "You ever think of what it would be like if we were both in *la Resistenza?* We'd care too much about each other, we'd jeopardize missions for each other, we'd want to risk our lives for each other. I'm eighteen, Mara, the soldiers would have come to my house anyway and told me that I needed to join the army, and what would I tell them? 'Sorry, officers, I can't, I'm a part of *la Resistenza.* Come back when the war's over.' Bet you ten thousand lira that wouldn't work."

He paused.

He was right.

Merda, he was right.

"Mara, look at me," Marco said, gripping my hand again, my eyes snapped up to his, "I love you, and I know you can't forgive me, even under the circumstances. I could have defied the government like you did, and joined you in *Napoli*. But I didn't. And maybe if I did, things would be different. But they aren't. Which is why I'm doing this. I'm trying to do the right thing here, to keep you safe. To protect you the way I couldn't when I was in *Roma*."

His eyes. They were beautiful.

They were the eyes I fell in love with.

But they were the eyes that broke my heart after I saw a photo of him, those same eyes looking happy, in that ENR uniform.

I couldn't forgive him, he was damn right about that.

But just because I couldn't forgive him, didn't mean I didn't still love him.

I did love him, but not in the way I did before. Now, I loved him in the way a friend would love a friend.

And that meant I had to protect him too.

"*Io capisco, Marco.* Listen, you can't go back to *Napoli*. It's not safe, the people are-"

"I have to, Mara."

"But-"

"I have to."

"*Perche?*"

"I just do," he said looking at the ground.

I knew why, I just didn't want to admit it, and it seemed that he didn't want to admit it either.

But he was a coward for not saying it out loud. He was ashamed of what he did, and yet here he was, still clinging to the ENR, at their beck and call, even if it meant he'd be turning against his countrymen.

I broke eye contact, looking straight ahead again, the people around me were overwhelming as they all talked in English. My mind couldn't keep up. It was too hard to understand what they were saying, all talking over each other, making it very difficult to concentrate on what Marco was saying.

"Filomena told me what happened yesterday," he whispered.

I jumped at how close his voice sounded, and my head snapped to the side. He was right next to me. Before there was space. Now there wasn't.

"Did she?" I said curtly, back to not tolerating him talking to me.

"Are you okay?"

I took a deep breath, trying to calm myself down to keep from yelling at him, but I couldn't stop the aggression coming through in my voice, "Marco, something you would have known had you not been a coward and joined the ENR, is when something like that happens, when you lose someone in that way, you take a second, pray, and thank *Dio* it wasn't you. I'm fine. *La Resistenza* will have casualties. I was aware of that when I signed up. I was signing up for possibly being tortured and killed like some of the people in *Roma*. I'm fine. Losing people is the price we have to pay for getting freedom."

"But you-"

"*Io bene, Marco. E tu?*" I shifted my eyes to him once again, but he was so close. Shoulder to shoulder, if not closer.

He let out a breath, "I don't know, Mara. The ENR, they're, they don't understand the word civilians. If you're in their way, you're out. And now everything is crumbling, Germany's invaded, the Allies have invaded, and everyone is freaking out."

I smirked, "That's what happens when you're on the

wrong side of the war."

"Mara, I could get killed."

"I could too. All those months, I could've gotten killed, but you didn't give a *merda*," I said, my voice level. I didn't raise it. I was afraid if I yelled, the whole world would be able to hear what I had to say.

He was about to speak but I stopped him, "No, Marco, we're done talking, because all of those months you could have sent a letter. You could have explained yourself. But you didn't. Because you're a coward. And that is one thing you and I will never have in common. You run from things, I fight them."

And that was the last of it. I looked at the people walking by and side stepped, putting distance between Marco and I once again.

As it should be.

Luca came back from getting a newspaper, and locked eyes with me, as if to ask, *What did I miss?*

A lot.

He came to stand in between me and Marco, which was a good decision, I was pretty sure I would have whipped my gun out of my suitcase and shot him point blank if Luca hadn't come in the way.

More people surged around us as we stood there.

I felt out of place in the station, like I should've been moving around as well. The women dressed a lot more vibrantly here, and their skirts were longer, and bigger. They wore hats and had heels on, while I was wearing boots and probably had pieces of straw in my knotted hair.

Another train raced into the station, halting by the platform and I watched as a station master came out of one of the side doors, "Train to Falmouth, Train to Falmouth," he yelled.

I nodded at Luca.

"That's us."

He grunted in response, grabbing his suitcase which had been placed against the wall behind us.

"You have your ticket?" I asked.

"Yes."

"And remember, let me do the talking."

I spoke English, Luca did not. Him trying to speak wouldn't get us far. And we were so close.

He nodded and we started to walk up to the coach. I turned my head to look at Marco one last time, who bobbed his head, as if to say, *go ahead.* I gave him a little two fingered salute, before going up to the station master.

"Ticket?" He asked quickly, so much so that I was taken aback trying to translate.

When I finally got it, I handed the piece of paper to him while Luca passed him his.

He looked at both of the tickets and then looked between Luca and I.

"You two're going to Falmouth?"

"Yes sir," I said in English, trying to make my voice as quiet as possible so he couldn't hear the accent.

"What's your business there?"

"Sightseeing, sir," I mumbled, almost robotically. Filomena had told me exactly what to say when the station master asked questions.

"It is a beautiful place."

I tried to smile but it was difficult trying to look natural and hide how my whole body was shaking, "That is what I've heard."

"Honeymoon?" He asked, motioning towards Luca.

Merda, I was never going to live this down.

I took Luca's hand, who looked surprised. He didn't understand what we were saying.

"That would be us."

"Hard time right now to have a honeymoon, can't travel out of the country."

I nodded, "Yes, but if this war has taught us anything, there is no time like the present."

The station master smiled, "Of course. Well you two go on now. Have a nice time."

"Thank you," I said before gripping Luca's hand even tighter, pulling him forward, up the steps and into the train. I let out a sigh of relief when we made it.

I quickly let go of Luca's hand and kept walking, him not that far behind me.

I found a smaller compartment, only for two people, and I smiled. Good.

I opened the door, and it slid open. Luca got in first and I followed, shutting the compartment afterward.

The seats were facing each other, just benches covered in fluff and fabric, and there was a window on the wall between them.

I plopped down on one side, Luca the other, we looked at each other for a minute.

"We made it," I breathed out.

Luca smiled, "*Si*, we did."

Silence for a second as the realization hit. It took three days of nonstop travel, sleeping for two hours at a time, all to get on this one train going to the middle of nowhere.

I locked eyes with Luca, "You should probably get some sleep, *Dio* knows we didn't get any rest while we were getting here."

He nodded, "You should as well."

I smiled, "I will." We both knew that was a lie.

In a few minutes, while people were still trying to find seats, Luca was out. Head against the wall of the train.

I couldn't sleep, my mind was racing a million kilometers a minute.

I leaned against the window, the glass cold against my cheek, and looked at the platform a few yards away.

I found Marco in the same place we'd left him. His green eyes stared at me as the train made a hissing sound.

It was the last time I would probably see him.

This was what defined us, what defined our last few minutes together.

So I did one thing I thought I'd never do.

As the train started to move away, I mouthed, *Ti perdono.*

I forgive you.

CHAPTER 3

September 28th, 1943, 6:13pm, Falmouth Station, Falmouth, Cornwall, England
James

"Papers, get your papers here! Allies invade Italy, gaining headway. Germans get caught up in the Italian civil war in Naples. Read all about it in today's paper, get it while you still can!"

A man walked up to me and put a shilling in the cup I had set out. I smiled my thanks as I handed him a paper from the stack.

The train station was still buzzing with life, even this late. People were getting back from day jobs farther away. Then there were the usual few who had nothing better to do than stay at the station.

"Papers! Hear the latest news from the front lines."

"James?" I heard a deep voice call, which made me abandon yelling about the war. Instead I turned my head towards where the voice was coming from.

Uncle George was standing in the doorway of the ticket booth where he had been sitting all day, selling tickets, sorting money, sending telegrams, and telling the few men who still worked at the station what to do.

"Yes?" I asked as I ran over to him.

"Pack up for the day, will you?"

"But we still have a few trains left, I can make a couple

pounds more with those."

He laughed, "I know, I know, but we best be starting to get ready to leave. We have visitors, you know."

I raised an eyebrow. No, I didn't know. "What do you mean, visitors?"

"Didn't your aunt tell you?"

I shook my head.

"Bloody hell, Hester," Uncle George said to himself before looking at me, "Well, we're welcoming-"

Before he could finish the whistle of a train screeched as it rolled into the small station, and Uncle George smiled that smile of his that always seemed to be on his face.

He was a happy man, always with a joke or ready to laugh at one. Kind as hell too. He'd offer a job to anyone who didn't have a place to go. Didn't matter if he didn't need any more workers at the time, he'd hire them just to give them a place to go to every day. But now it seemed that there weren't enough people just standing around looking for work. Everyone had gone off to fight in the war, leaving my uncle with endless amounts of repairs and work to be done. I'd offered my help, but he knew that I couldn't do much. I wasn't very good at heavy lifting or repairing things. I ended up doing much more harm than good.

Uncle George's hair was greying rapidly, but that didn't matter, he'd told me as long as his blue eyes, just like mine, were filled with life, he was still kicking.

He looked at the train, "Well, you'll just have to see for yourself, that's their train."

The train hit a stop in front of the platform, and the doors started to open, with the station master and other workers stepping out, and setting up the stairs that led down from the train.

People started to trickle out. The women were helped down by their male counterparts, or by the men holding the door. I watched a few of the men thank the workers for what they did, one or two tossed them shillings or pence. Just as it seemed like there was no one else on the train, two more people made their way out.

Young people, one girl and one boy.

She was wearing boots and a matching skirt and shirt-jacket, and he was wearing a wrinkled short sleeve button up with long pants, same as me, but while I was wearing a vest over it, he wasn't. In fact a few of the buttons on his shirt were undone, and it billowed a little.

Their skin was tan where mine was pale. The girl's brown hair was pulled up with a ribbon, the sides pinned, while the boy's, similar in color, had no pomade in it. The hair that would have been plastered to his head swooped down and fell into his eyes as he walked.

Each of them had a small leather suitcase.

The boy walked down first, nodding towards the train worker, and the girl followed. When the worker held out his hand to help her down she shook her head and jumped off the train, ignoring the steps, landing on the platform with ease.

They looked around, staring at the small outdoor station in awe, as if they had never seen one like it before.

I looked at Uncle George who was eyeing the two people.

"What?" I asked.

"I believe that's them," he said, starting to make his way over to two complete strangers.

"Uncle George, what are you talking about?"

"Just follow me, James."

He walked up to the two of them, who looked completely lost, and flashed a smile.

"Cheao, como stay?" He asked in one of the most broken foreign languages in the entire world.

The girl chuckled a little, "I speak English," she said with a heavy foreign accent, "You don't have to try to speak. But thank you."

Her thank bordered on sounding like tank.

Uncle George shifted his attention to the boy, and so did I. He was looking straight at me.

"And what about you, do you speak English?"

The boy was silent, which made the girl laugh, "No, he doesn't."

Uncle George smiled, "Well, welcome to Falmouth. My name's George Smithson."

The girl nodded, "Pleasure to meet you, Mr. Smithson. My name is Mara, and this is Luca."

She then turned to Luca and started speaking quickly, "*Il suo nome e George Smithson.*"

Luca nodded and looked at Uncle George, "Ello," he said, trying to force the word out.

Mara's eyes shifted to me, "Who are you?" she asked abruptly, as if I wasn't quite trustworthy until I told her.

"Uh, James, Smithson. I'm his nephew. Pleasure to meet you," I said quickly, my words all meshing together.

She gave a sheepish smile, "James, my English isn't *that* good, could you talk slower?"

I felt my cheeks grow hot as I repeated myself. She nodded.

"Pleasure to meet you too," she said, holding out her hand.

I shook it, and took note of the rough calluses that laiden her palms.

She then looked at Luca, and once again translated. Luca's hazel eyes, the same ones as Mara's locked with mine.

They were amazing eyes.

"Ello, James," he said, trying to force every word out of his mouth again.

"Hello," I said, before holding out my hand for him to shake, he did, and I felt the same calluses were on his skin.

"Uh, forgive me, but uh, why are you here?" I asked, voicing the question that had been pounding into my head.

Mara blinked, "We are a part of *la Resistenza* in *Italia*, but our commanders felt it would be safer if we were away from the violence that is coming. If you haven't heard, we are on the verge of, erm, what you English people call 'civil war.' And your uncle has been kind enough to open his home to us."

My gaze flickered over to Uncle George who just shrugged, "I thought Hester would have told you about them."

"Well, obviously not," I mumbled.

They were Italian.

Bloody hell.

They were from Italy.

Uncle George looked between us, "Alright, come on then, we need to get back to the house before it's dark out, or your aunt will have my head."

He smiled at the two Italians, "You're going to love Hester, she's quite a lovely person, wonderful cook too."

Mara smiled back. Uncle George motioned for us to follow him and she did quite quickly, lugging her suitcase without a problem, Luca right behind her.

I watched as they both started off, and let out a breath.

What the bloody hell had my Uncle gotten himself

into?

Luca

The road was bumpy and it made the back of the coach bob up and down with every rock in the road. I was sitting next to Mara, who was reading the newspaper I had gotten back in Plymouth, her brow furrowed in concentration. James, I think that was his name, was on the other side facing us. Mr. Smithson was at the front, guiding the horses.

They had horses.

Horses.

I'd already named one Dante, and the other Guiseppe.

The coach was a simple farming wagon that I'd used in the past to carry equipment in during the harvest. It was wooden, and the back had been closed with two boards nailed into it. The only ways to get out were small openings on either side.

I looked up to catch James looking at me again. I had felt his eyes on me since we'd gotten in the coach.

I kept sneaking glances at him. Every so often, one of us would catch the other staring and we'd look away. He looked German, that was the first thought that rushed through my head. The blonde hair, the ocean blue eyes, and the skin that made Mara and I look like coal.

After James caught me looking at him once again, I resolved to just stare to the sides. It was easier that way, I didn't want him to keep catching me, and then have him ask why I was looking at him. I didn't think it was polite to say, 'I was looking at you because you look like a *Nazista*.'

Yes, that would go over well.

The rolling fields of the country were just how I'd pictured them.

Green. Very green.

And not the kind of hills I was used to. No. Our hills back in *Abruzzo* were steep, and almost mountains. They would have been if it wasn't for the lush vineyards that sat on top of rich soil. These hills were small, they were like waves in a green sea, and the cobblestone walls that divided the road and the fields weren't like anything I'd seen before. In *Abruzzo* there were barely fences to determine who had what land. You just knew. And the sky, the sky was a murky dusk, clouds covered it, which wasn't something I was used to. The setting sun gave the fields a golden glow and as I was looking around, my eyes caught on something.

A house.

A beautiful white one off in the distance which we kept getting closer to. It was on a cliff, I couldn't see any land past that point. Off to the side, there were wooden steps that looked like they led straight down the cliff.

My eyes found something else as I looked past the house.

Blue.

L'oceano

The ocean.

My jaw slowly started to drop as we got closer to not only the house, but the beautiful blue expanse beyond it.

I nudged Mara and she bolted up as if she had been in a trance. She furrowed her brow in confusion and I pointed out the view. We were on the cliff now, looking down onto the ocean and the sand banks below.

Her eyes widened, "*Merda*," she breathed out.

Merda was right.

The coach stopped right in front of the giant house, making the back lurch a little with the lack of motion.

Mr. Smithson looked back at us, "We're here."

Mara looked at me and translated, "*Siamo qui.*"

Oh. Okay.

Wait, what?

This was where we were staying?

Compared to where Mara and I had been living back in *Napoli,* this was a mansion.

I nodded at Mr. Smithson, as if to tell him I understood.

He abandoned his post in the front with the horses, and instead came to the back to help us.

Mr. Smithson held out his hand to Mara to give her assistance, "Lady's first."

I didn't understand what he was saying, but judging by how Mara's eyes darkened with anger for a second before they returned to their calm hazel again, it probably was something that made her out to be different from the three men she was around.

For as long as I'd known Mara, she was always doing things by herself. Anything from farm work to fixing the house she lived in when her father couldn't get out of bed. But sometimes, she pretended like she couldn't do all of those things. She found it best not to argue or protest, and just go along with it. Besides, a girl who was capable, was dangerous.

At least that's what Mara had said once.

I had never understood it. If she was able to do work that some men couldn't, why wouldn't she flaunt it?

She took Mr. Smithson's hand with a smile and walked down the steps hesitantly, even though I knew she would have jumped down from them if Mr. Smithson wasn't there. Judging by James's look of confusion, he probably wondered why she hadn't. I was convinced he'd seen us get off the train and Mara jumping onto the platform.

Once she was down, Mr. Smithson started walking away, leaving me with James the Nazi. Maybe it wasn't the best name for him, but, there were a lot of James' in England, had to set him apart somehow.

I stepped towards the opening at the same time as he did, and we ran into each other.

I let out a grunt and backed up, "Sorry," I muttered, knowing that it didn't sound like sorry.

He flashed me a smile, one that knocked the breath out of my lungs, "*Sei bene.*"

You're good.

Wait, what?

James laughed a little at my wide eyed expression, shaking his head, gesturing for me to go first but I shook my head. He could go.

"*Grazie.*"

I nodded, "*Prego.*"

And that was where I lost him, his eyebrow raised in confusion.

He stepped down, gingerly going down each step. Once he had cleared them, I smirked and went to the edge, jumping down. I landed in the rocky path and my boot slipped on the gravel, making me stumble, but two hands came around my torso to stop me from falling.

James.

I looked up at him as he tilted me upright. His hands were on me, on my chest, right over where my shirt was unbuttoned. My breath caught in my throat again as I locked eyes with him. I was drowning in the blue, in the way his hands felt like fire on my skin.

"*Dannazione,*" I muttered.

Damn.

James kept looking at me, and we must have looked like *idioti*. But his touch, the heat, the ocean.

And then the feeling was gone, destroyed when he pulled his hands away as if he'd just burned himself.

He cleared his throat, "Sorry."

I didn't know what to say.

What could I say?

What could I say in English?

Nothing.

"*Mi dispiace,*" I said in *Italiano* as if I had lost the ability to think.

I'm sorry.

James held his arm out, clearly not understanding what I was trying to say, and gestured towards the house. I nodded. Mara and Mr. Smithson had already disappeared inside, the door still open.

At least they hadn't forgotten about us.

James led the way, and I couldn't help watching his stride as he walked towards the house, and then something hit me like an anvil.

Porca Merda.

What the *fanculo* just happened?

Mara

Luca walked into the house finally, a little red in the face, "Took you long enough, *fratello.*"

"Sorry," he breathed out before looking around the entrance to the house.

It was a huge space. Wood floors that shone, and wallpaper that wasn't peeling. The openness of the entryway made me let out a sigh of relief. I hated small spaces.

Mr. Smithson looked at Luca and I gaping and laughed, "Well don't just stand there, come in, come in," he said, motioning for us to walk farther into the house.

All three of us, Luca, James, and I advanced. There was a staircase to the right that was beautifully painted an off-white color, however, it didn't look like the sturdiest thing in the world. And farther still I could see the kitchen, the living room, and the dining room, all through separate doorways. Not any doors though.

"Hester, we're home," Mr. Smithson called.

"Who's we?" A voice yelled from somewhere in the kitchen. It was light and high, a woman.

"Me, James, and the two people you forgot to tell James about."

"They're here?"

"Yes."

Someone emerged from the kitchen, an older woman who gave Luca and I a warm smile.

"Hello you two, I'm Mrs. Smithson, that one's wife," she gestured to Mr. Smithson next to us.

She didn't speak slowly, but she didn't speak fast either, it was calming. Peaceful.

I smiled, "Pleasure to meet you, Mrs. Smithson, My name is Mara, and this is Luca."

"Your English is very good, Mara."

My chest heated up with pride, "Thank you."

Mrs. Smithson clapped her hands together, "Now, let's get you two settled in. Come on, follow me, you too James."

She futzed with her blonde hair as she flew up the stairs and we all followed behind her.

We got to the first door and she smiled, "Mara this will be your room."

Wait, what?

She opened the door, and I peered in.

It was huge.

A bed was perched in the right hand corner, and off to the left was a dresser and mirror, a bookshelf was against the wall towards the back, right next to a window.

The window was wider, a large bench situated under it and set into the wall.

The room was beautiful.

I slowly walked in and spun around facing Luca, who was smiling at me.

"*La mia stanza*," I said, looking at Luca.

My own room.

Mrs. Smithson laughed, "You look like you've never seen a room before, Mara."

I turned to look at her, "I haven't had my own room in a very long time."

She blinked, "Oh, well, I'm glad that you get one now," she let out a breath and continued, "We'll let you get settled in while I show your boyfriend where he's staying."

I raised an eyebrow, "Um, forgive me, Mrs. Smithson, but what is boyfriend?" I asked.

"Uh, you and Luca are, uh," She interlocked her two hands.

I still didn't understand.

Then she held out a finger as if she had got an idea of what to do. She made her hands into mini faces, and then made the tips of her fingers touch, as if they were kissing.

Wait.

Boy.

Friend.

Kissing.

Oh.

"Oh, no, no, no. No, we're not," I chuckled a little, "One moment, Luca looks confused."

I then turned to Luca who had his eyebrows raised, wondering what all the no's were for.

"She thinks we're together," I said, trying to stifle a laugh.

He blinked, before laughing, "No."

I switched back to English, "No, we're not together, he's almost my *fratello*. Uh, my brother."

Mrs. Smithsons face turned red. She was embarrassed, "Oh, well, your brother, I'll show your brother where he'll be staying."

I nodded and watched as Mrs. Smithson motioned for Luca and James to walk with her.

As soon as they were gone, I couldn't help myself from smiling.

I had a room.

I walked- No, I ran over to where the window was, and plopped down on the bench, looking out the glass. My eyes took in the view of the blue ocean that expanded out for kilometers.

It was beautiful.

I'd always been close to the sea in *Abruzzo*. We were right by it after all, but there was something different about this side of the ocean. It was restless. Wild.

I let out a sigh, unfolding the newspaper in my hand and started reading the front page for the second time.

Italy Is Invaded!

Wow, what a great title...

CHAPTER 4

**September 29th, 1943, 12:14am Falmouth,
Cornwall, England
Mara**

I was wide awake, my body buzzing with a need to
be somewhere else as I stared up at sky blue wallpaper,
counting how many pink roses there were.

How long had I been up?

The moon was shining high in the sky and filled my
dark room with an eerie white light, and I knew it had
been at least a few hours since the Smithsons had eaten
dinner. I hadn't eaten much, deciding to take some bread
up to my room after everyone else had finished. It had
been quiet at the table, and Luca had barely touched his
food either. Mrs. Smithson tried to hide her hurt, but I
knew she felt offended we didn't eat. It wasn't that we
didn't want to, we just weren't used to it.

With *la Resistenza* I learned very quickly that my stomach needed to get used to not eating. And now that I was
used to not eating, my body was convinced I didn't need
to.

Knock knock knock.

My eyes snapped to the door, "*Che cosa?*"

"It's me."

Luca.

"Come in."

The door swung open to reveal Luca standing there in pajamas, the only set he actually owned. They were a mess, dirt covered the knees and collar, holes dotted the set, and half the top was unbuttoned.

Habit of his.

I myself was wearing almost the exact same ensemble as him. Cotton pants, and a collared shirt. The only difference was mine didn't unbutton.

I had taken my hair down from the ponytail and made the ribbon that I'd used to tie it up into a headband.

"*Como stai?*" I asked.

He shrugged as he made his way into the room. I sat up on the bed and motioned for him to sit down next to me.

"Eh."

"What's that supposed to mean?"

He turned his head so that he could look at me, "I don't know, Mara. This is just, odd."

"Yes, it is. They seem nice enough, but..." I trailed off.

"It's odd having people be nice."

I nodded, "Yeah."

We sat in silence for a minute, the weight of our distrust of others a familiar feeling on our shoulders.

"So, what do you think of your room?" Luca asked, gesturing around us.

"Big."

He laughed a little, "Yeah, it is."

"What do you think of yours?"

"It'd be better if my roommate actually spoke my language."

I handed him the newspaper that'd been laying at the edge of the bed, "Here take this."

"Why?"

"See if you can read it."

He gave it a once over and huffed, "Mara, it's in English."

I shrugged, "Well, then I guess you won't be able to figure out what the Allies are doing in Italy. Your loss."

"You're evil."

"Maybe," I smirked.

Luca smiled, looking over to the other side of the room, "We made it. You realize that right? We're safe."

I got up from the bed and made my way over to the window seat, looking through the glass to check if anyone was watching me, before sitting down.

"Sometimes being safe doesn't matter," I said, my voice hushed.

"Mara..."

"I'm just saying, I'd rather be fighting."

"Would you rather die at the hands of a German?" he snapped.

"I'd rather not run from my problems like you are so happy to do," I clapped back.

"So what do you call whatever the hell happened between you and Marco?"

I opened my mouth to speak, but closed it again.

"We sorted everything out."

"No, before. When you found out. The Mara I know would have marched right into *Roma* and kicked him in the balls. But you didn't. You couldn't even stay in *Abruzzo* after it, so you went to *la Resistenza* in *Napoli*. You ran."

I huffed, "That's different."

"Is it?"

Luca was giving me that face, the *I'm right and you're wrong* one that made me want to scream.

"Yes, it is. Besides, what are we even going to do here?"

He shrugged, "Well, Mara, we're in the country by an

ocean. Maybe read a book, sleep, go for a walk."

I let out a groan and flopped back onto the bed making it bounce as I laid back, "That sounds boring," I whined.

"Anything that doesn't involve *la Resistenza,* violence, or potentially dying is boring to you."

My arm flew up and snapped before pointing at him, "Correct."

"Well, I'm going to walk around the beach a lot."

I huffed, "Suit yourself, I'm going to be trying to figure out how to get out of here."

"But you have your own room, why would you want to leave this?"

I paused for a second. That was true...

"You know what, you should probably get to sleep, *fratello,* we have a whole day tomorrow of lounging around pretending to do something with our lives in one of the most peaceful places in the world."

"You do realize their capital is getting leveled, right?" Luca asked as he got up from the bed.

"And you do realize our country's heading into a civil war, has a fascist dictator, and both sides of the biggest war in history are invading us? I think we've got them beat."

Luca paused for a second and thought about it, "Good point." His mouth opened slightly in a yawn, before looking back at me, "Right, and that's my cue to go back to my room and get some sleep."

I smiled a little, "You do that," I mumbled.

"You should too."

"I'll sleep when I want to."

"If you had your way you'd never sleep."

"Who said I ever slept in the first place? What if I figured out how to survive without it?"

Luca smirked, "That would explain the extreme aggression."

I laughed a little, "Oh no, those are my good days."

"Then how are you on a bad day?" he asked, raising an eyebrow.

I stopped to think for a second, "Uh... Oh, I got it. The day I found out Marco left for *Roma*."

Luca blinked, and then blinked again, remembering what happened that day.

"You shot a cow."

"And?"

"That's your bad day?"

"Yes."

I did everything *but* march all the way to *Roma* and kick him in the balls that day.

"So if you have a bad day-"

I sat up a little, "Who knows, maybe I'll kill the *Nazista* in your room," I said, raising an eyebrow.

He laughed a little to himself, "Please don't, he's too attractive."

Wait, what?

"Che diavolo hai detto?"

What the hell did you say?

"Uh, you know, I wouldn't want the girls to miss him."

I chuckled a little, "He's not that good looking."

"Really? You don't think so?"

"There's nothing to him, he's just, eh," I said, shrugging.

Luca scoffed, "Eh? He's eh?"

I put my hands up in surrender, "Look, he's not my type."

"Yeah, your type has green eyes, tan skin, sandy brown hair, and likes to stab people in the back," he said with a smirk.

My jaw dropped as he made a break for the door.

"*Vaffanculo, tu cazzo!*" I called, a smile on my face.

Funny how I now laughed about what Marco did. At least, I did with Luca. The door closed, and I was left alone again.

I leaned back and just stared at the ceiling.

I felt vulnerable like this, in a house with no protection.

No one's gonna come after you.

No one's gonna kill you.

No one wants to hurt you.

No one even knows you exist here.

And even though all that was true, I still went over to my suitcase that was situated on top of the dresser, pulled out my pistol, and slipped it under my pillow.

Just because I thought I was safe, didn't mean I was.

James

My eyes fluttered back and forth across the first page of the book, reading about how a man named Lee Chong owned a grocery store. Why it was important? I had absolutely no idea.

The door swung open, and I reflexively hid the book behind me.

My uncle didn't exactly like John Steinbeck.

Said he was insane, that his books would mess with my head.

This was the second time I was reading *Cannery Row*, and I was slowly starting to believe Uncle George. This guy was all over the place. I wasn't reading it a second time for fun, I was reading it because I had no clue what the bloody hell was going on the first time around.

I mean, he talked about gophers for a whole chapter.

I knew it was a metaphor, but really?

Gophers?

Couldn't he have come up with something better than a gopher?

Someone cleared their throat in my room.

In my room, in the middle of the night, when I was trying to decide if what I was reading was important.

My eyes looked up at who it was.

Shirt unbuttoned, barefoot, messed up dark hair that fell in his face.

Luca.

My breath hitched.

"*Ciao*," he said with a smile.

I waved a little before shakily opening the book once again. Reading about the stores hours this time.

"*Cosa stai leggendo?*"

My eyes snapped back to Luca, who was now sitting on the other bed in the room, only a few feet from mine, separated by a night stand.

"Uh, what?"

He chuckled and pointed towards the book in my hand.

"Oh, uh, it's *Cannery Row* by John Steinbeck."

A wave of confusion came over his face, but he nodded, "Oh."

I smiled, but didn't say anything more. I didn't know if I could say more.

What does a person say to someone who doesn't speak their language?

I watched him crawl into bed, and turn so he was facing me. When he finally closed his eyes, I started reading again.

"James?" he whispered.

"Yes?"

"*Bouna notte.*"

Good night.

The words rolled off his tongue melodically.

I nodded my response, going back to the weird lives of the people on Cannery Row.

"James?" Luca said again.

His voice was like honey when he said my name, and I found myself wanting to hear him say it over and over again. I wanted to memorize how beautiful it sounded when he said it.

"Yes?"

He propped himself up on his elbow, "*Come si dice-?*" Luca then went on to point at the book in my hand.

How do you say...

Oh.

I held up the book, "Book."

"*Libro,*" he responded with a smile.

"*Libro,*" I repeated.

"Book," the word on his tongue sounded more like a ghost saying boo, and then adding the k after.

"*Bene,*" I said smiling.

Luca's mouth turned upwards as well, returning to a sitting position on his bed, mirroring me.

His cotton shirt was unbuttoned half way, and the fabric billowed out, exposing the upper part of his torso. I must have been staring because he cleared his throat, which snapped my gaze back to his face.

His eyes were filled with confusion as he looked back down at his chest, trying to figure out what was wrong with it, "*Che cosa?*"

I blinked and shook my head, "Nothing."

Luca didn't understand what I was saying so he just shrugged, ignoring me as he lied back down on the bed.

He wasn't under the blanket and I could see his shoulders rise and fall with his breathing. The moon illuminated the room and cast a white light against Luca's face making him look at ease.

He looked peaceful, handsome ev-

What the bloody hell was I thinking?

I was tired.

I was reading John Steinbeck.

That explained it.

I snuck one more glance at Luca. His lips slightly parted, hair falling into his eyes, shirt starting to hang off his shoulders.

My breath hitched and I felt my stomach get lighter.

I shook my head, snapping myself out of whatever the bloody hell that was.

CHAPTER 5

**September 29th, 1943, 2:23am Falmouth,
Cornwall, England**
Mara

Running. Faster and faster.
Cobblestone.
Grenades in my pockets.
Safehouse.
Gunshot.
Gunshot.
Gunshot.
BANG!
Screams.
Amelia.
Blood, everywhere.
My hands were covered in blood.
Was I bleeding?
Where was I?

I looked around me, I was in the middle of *Napoli*, surrounded by a pool of blood. My boots were drenched in it.

There were bodies all around me, some I recognized as
a part of *la Resistenza,* others I didn't.

They looked like locals.

Blood dripped from their mouths, gunshot wounds to
the torso, the head, the chest.

What was going on?

I felt the need to run again, even though it felt like my lungs were going to burst as it was.

I'd been running for a while.

But why, and from what, I did not know.

I took off again, sprinting through the pool of blood, making it slosh up and stain the bare skin of my legs. I kept running, but I didn't get very far before my boots, wet with blood, slipped on the smooth cobblestone, and I found myself starting to fall.

I couldn't catch myself, and plummeted into the dark liquid.

I tried to get up, but everytime I did, I tumbled back down.

Everytime I fell, the pool of blood got deeper.

I was sinking.

It filled my mouth, my nose, it got in my eyes.

All I could taste was metal, and all I could smell was death.

I was flailing around in the blood, trying to get back to the surface.

It was dark in the pool, maroon. No air. I was drowning.

I swam to the surface, and let out a gasp, reaching out for the cobblestone in front of me.

My hands gripped the uneven street as I started to pull myself up.

And then I heard footsteps.

"*Ciao, Mara.*"

I could see two shiny black boots, and when my eyes moved upwards, they came into contact with two green irises.

Marco.

"*Marco, aiutami per favore,*" I gasped as I started coughing up blood that wasn't mine.

Please help me.

He smiled that smile that I remember him always having.

But this time there was something more to it. It was scary this time. Hollow.

"*Mi dispiace, Mara,* I can't do that."

"*Perche?*"

"You're with *la Resistenza.*"

"And?"

I saw his hand go to grab something in his waistband, a gun, pointing it at my head.

Fanculo.

"*Marco, per favore. Non farlo.*"

"*Mi dispiace, Mara.* I'm just following orders. *Ti amo.*"

He cocked the gun, placing his finger on the trigger.

"*Marc-*"

BANG!

My head burned as blood trickled down my face. The shock of the blast, and the pain that came after it made me lose my grip on the cobblestone. I fell back into the pool of blood, only this time, mine was in there too.

I felt everything going dark.

My eyes snapped open, and I shot up in bed. Reflexively, I reached for the gun under my pillow, turning the safety off, cocking the gun, and pointing it in front of me.

The room was dark.

The moon was still high in the sky.

I was drenched in sweat and breathing heavily as if I was hyperventilating.

There was no one here.

I was in England, not *Italia.*

I was in my room.

I was safe.

My hands were trembling as I slowly lowered my gun, putting it back under the pillow.

I ran a hand through my damp hair and let out a shaky breath as I slowly lowered myself back down onto the bed.

I was safe.

I was fine.

I was alive.

I wasn't in *Italia* anymore.

There were no *Nazisti*. There were no ENR soldiers.

No one was going to hurt me.

But when I tried to close my eyes again, all I could see was Marco pointing the barrel of the gun at me.

I couldn't go back to sleep.

If I did, I was afraid I'd be right back where I was.

Dying in an ocean of blood.

I exhaled a long breath before throwing the blanket off me and jumping out of bed.

I needed air.

I slipped my boots on and readjusted the ribbon in my hair to turn into a ponytail.

If I went down the stairs, someone would hear me. Those stairs were as rickety as the ones at the safe house and I didn't want to explain to one of the Smithsons that I needed to get air because I was having horrible nightmares.

That would only get me pity, and I didn't need anyone's pity.

I wanted to be respected because I fought for the rights of freedom in a way that no one in England could ever dream of.

I wanted to be respected because I did things that most people my age would cower away from.

I wanted to be respected because I had seen so much, and had never let it cloud my judgement.

Pity didn't get anyone respect, pity made Luca and I the poor Italians who escaped.

I looked out the window.

Don't you even think about it.

Too late.

I went over to the glass and looked down. The house was two stories. I could easily jump down and land in the bushes that surrounded the house or climb down as much as I could, then drop.

Or I could improvise.

Don't improvise.

I'm gonna improvise.

I unlocked the window and opened it, letting it swing out. The smell of salt flowed through the air, overpowering the lingering scent of blood from my dream. A cold breeze blew into the room, ruffling my hair a little.

I was about to swing my legs over when another gust of cold air came into the room, making me shiver.

It was really cold.

I backed away from the window and went to my suitcase, prying it open. My eyes scanned over the clothes and easily found my thick brown coat. The only one I owned.

It had large pockets, and could have been buttoned up almost all the way to the collar, but I preferred to keep it open. There was a belt as well that hung loosely around the coat, kept in place by three loops that staggered themselves on the right, left and back of the coat. It was worn, and in some places the fabric was threadbare, but I hadn't needed it often back home so I'd never thought to get another one.

I slipped my arms into it and adjusted the coat against

the cotton of my pajama set.

My hands were still shaking, so I grabbed the one thing that I knew would steady them. My hand tightened around the gun before dropping it into the coat pocket.

Just in case.

I went to the window and swung my legs over the side, the cold pricking my skin through the cotton pajamas.

Are you sure about this?

Yes.

I shifted, clutching the windowsill tightly, and once I felt I had a good hold, I looked over to the side.

Ivy was climbing up the side of the house, thick and green, intertwining and running this way and that.

I smirked, wondering if James had ever snuck out of the house like this before.

I slid off the sill, and let my hands keep me from falling as I hung from the window.

My feet dangled in the air and I moved my hands, inching towards the right where the ivy was creeping up the walls.

Once I reached the end of the windowsill, I snuck a glance at the ivy.

This better work.

And if it doesn't?

I paused for a second.

Uh, this better work.

I moved my right hand off the sill, and then started reaching for the vines. When I found a good hold, I gripped it and swung my right foot over as well, where it caught on a large knot of ivy.

I let out a breath.

Now the hard part.

I tightened my hold on the vines, and pushed off the

window, my left hand flailing to get a hold on something. When I grasped an uneven wood plank on the side of the house and secured my foot next to the other one already there, I let out a sigh of relief. I hadn't plummeted to my death yet.

I started to climb down the side of the house, one foot after the other, until my boots brushed the ground. Placing my other foot down and released the ivy, I brushed off my hands as I started walking.

I could hear the ocean roaring beyond the cliff. The scent of salt got stronger as I made my way towards the stairs that led to the sandy banks. I wrapped my coat tight around me as the sea breeze worked its way through my clothes and into my skin, making me shiver.

The stairs creaked, and in one or two places they wobbled, as if all of a sudden they were going to give out from under me and send me down to the sharp rocks below. I'd hit my head, pass out, and no one would find me until morning, probably already dead.

But that was the worst case scenario.

I quickened my pace going down the steps, hoping that the faster I got off them, the less likely I was to die trying to get down to the beach.

When I finally got to the bottom, my boots sunk into the sand.

I took a second to inhale the salt air. It calmed me down a bit, but the image of Marco with a gun to my head kept playing in the back of my mind. The pool of blood, me drowning, choking on the red liquid.

My hand went to my pocket, where the gun was.

That was my lifeline. It was my tether. It made me feel safe, like nothing bad could happen.

The metal was frigid against my already cold hands,

but I didn't care.

My eyes were trained on the horizon: the dark sky and the even darker blue blanket that reached out for kilometers.

Maybe someone in *Italia* was standing on the beach in *Pescara* looking out into the expanse too.

Maybe we were looking at the same moon in the sky.

Maybe we were on the same side of the war.

Maybe we weren't.

Maybe that sand was coated in blood.

Maybe the beach was laden with bodies.

Or maybe, it was just a normal beach, nothing to suggest the country it belonged to was slowly becoming the next battleground of the war.

I picked up a piece of wood laying in the sand, and threw it. It arched in the air, landing in the water. The tide had brought the water closer to the steps and it would have taken me three steps forward to make my feet touch water.

I dug my boots into the sand, kicking it up as I started walking away from the steps. Up the shoreline.

My body was in England, but my mind was back home.

Not in *Napoli,* that wasn't my home.

Guardiagrele, Abruzzo was my home.

A small coastal region made up of small mountain towns with barely any transportation. I had to walk everywhere.

But it was my home.

Until it was occupied by *Nazista.*

We lost so much to them.

So when I left to go to *Napoli,* it wasn't like I was leaving my home. It was like I was leaving a town I'd never truly known. I hoped there would be a day when I could go back to that small village and have it feel like home once again. But with how the war was going, I didn't know. I'd be shocked if *Italia* was *Italia* by the end of the war.

My eyes were trained on the sand.

Padre Alberto, the priest at the church I went to before the Germans occupied the town and killed him, had once said to me when I was little that God knew the number of hairs on my head and how many grains of sand were on the beach. So when I went to the beach shortly after with my parents, I tried to count the grains of sand.

I spent hours trying to count, but by the time my parents told me it was time to go, I'd only counted a handful.

I'd thought, *if God could count all the grains of sand in the universe, he must be a very smart man.*

But then the war started, and everything I believed about God changed.

He wasn't a smart man.

He was a coward.

I'd stopped walking, and found myself a couple hundred yards away from the steps. The cliffs had smoothed out, and had turned into small hills, green grass on top of them.

The ocean was restless, whitecaps rolling in, churning the water.

And then it stopped.

The ocean stilled, and if only for a moment, the wind calmed to a gentle breeze.

And that's when I heard it.

Plink, plunk, ploonk.

Three circular ripples appeared in the water.

Che cosa?

My eyes darted to the left, where I had come from,

nothing.

And then they shifted to the right, and I saw a figure only a few yards away.

It was a man. Or a boy?

He was tall, at least taller than me. In the moonlight I could see him looking at me as my hair blew in the wind, light cotton pants rustling.

He smiled.

It was one of those smiles I was used to getting from boys back in *Abruzzo*. Charming.

He was charming.

"What's got you out this time of night?" he called. His voice was rough, a different diction than what James had. Where the Smithson household had voices that could have passed for royalty, this guy had a voice a chimney sweep would have. Like Bert from P.L. Travers' novels, he spoke with a Cockney accent.

I could barely understand what he was saying.

Though, my brain wasn't in the mood for translating normal English, much less Cockney English.

I wasn't going to respond.

"Can you 'ear me?"

I stayed silent.

I heard sand moving, and my eyes snapped up to where he had been, only to find him a few steps closer to me.

He smiled. It was infectious. It was the kind of smile you wanted to get from someone when you weren't feeling well. I'd just had a dream about being shot by my ex and drowning in an ocean of blood. At the moment, I needed someone to smile like that.

"'Ello," he said.

I nodded a greeting.

"Oh, come on, I don't even get a 'ello back? Am I that

ugly?"

I couldn't stop myself from smirking.

"I can't even see your face, how would I know if you were ugly?" I said, trying to hide my accent as much as possible, which was difficult in itself, muchless trying to get out full sentences.

"Fair enough."

Pause.

"So, what brings you out 'ere on this fine night, eh?"

I only could keep up with some of what he was saying.

I just shrugged. My mind was somewhere else.

The only thing that was breaking the silence between the two of us was the waves crashing onto the sand.

"Come on, woman, I'm really tryin' 'ere, you gotta give me some kind of answer. You're on a beach with a coat, your pajamas, and leather boots I'm pretty sure 'ave blood on 'em."

I looked down instinctively.

My shoes had blood on them?

From when?

Then it hit me.

When we'd left the safe house, they hadn't cleaned up the blood in the street from Amelia's death.

I must have stepped in it.

The guy continued, "I don't know if I should be concerned or not."

I huffed, shaking my head a little, I shouldn't be talking to this guy.

If I slipped up or he got the idea that I was from somewhere else I didn't know how he'd react.

I'd heard of people who were brutal towards immigrants and people who came from different countries. I'd heard about Japanese immigrants getting put in camps in America, and people like me were called names, some people denied them jobs, thinking they were spies.

I was scared this guy would try to do something more than just call me a few names.

But I got the impression that if I didn't talk to him, he wouldn't leave me alone.

I shifted my eyes to him, "Couldn't sleep."

He smiled, "Me neither. Nightmares."

"Me too," I muttered.

He shrugged, "Yeah, they can get to you, but they're just dreams."

I nodded, "Yes, they are."

"Goin' on walks 'elps me. Must 'elp you too, huh?"

"Yes, they do."

I sized him up, his dark hair hung down onto his forehead, casting an odd shadow across his face. He was wearing long pants cuffed at the bottom, and a button up shirt, rolled up at the sleeves, and the first few buttons undone, exposing the top of an undershirt.

He smiled at me, "You don't talk much do you?"

"Not to people I do not know," I said with a laugh.

"Well, the name's Will. Yours?"

"Mara," I replied shortly.

"Mara, huh?" He looked out at the ocean, "Mara," pause, "Mara. That's a beautiful name, Mara."

"Thank you," was all I could manage to say as he kept smiling at me.

"Well, now we know each other's names, we officially know each other."

"I don't think that is how it works."

He chuckled, "No, it's exactly 'ow it works. Says right 'ere in the knowin' someone contract."

It took me a few seconds to translate, eyebrows furrowed in concentration, but then I got it.

Will must have thought I was confused by what he said, because he held out his palm, pointing to one of the lines on his skin, "See right there, it says once you know someone's name, you know 'em," he paused for a second, looking up at me, "Life's too short these days Mara, you gotta know people, especially now."

I nodded, glancing back to the ocean, the moon was lowering itself towards the water. The sun would start to show itself soon.

"I need to go," I said, my accent slipping through a little bit more than I'd like.

Will looked surprised at my abruptness, but the corners of his mouth turned upward ever so slightly.

"You do that."

I started to turn around and leave but his voice stopped me, "'Ey, Mara?"

"*Che co-*" I stopped myself from saying anymore.

Merda.

But Will didn't seem to notice, or he didn't care enough to ask about my slip up, instead he just locked eyes with me, "'Ope to run into you again sometime. Perhaps not at night when we're runnin' away from nightmares."

I smiled my response before spinning and making my way back towards the steps and back to the house.

One thing was for certain, that walk did nothing to clear my head.

I still had the image of blood on my hands stuck in my mind, and the revelation of Amelia's staining my shoes wasn't helping.

I'd come to the conclusion that I'd left a bit of myself in *Italia,* and in *Napoli.* That was the part of me that believed everything was going to be okay. Will had a look in his eye when he was talking about "these days" that I was all too familiar with. It was a look that I saw too often when the *Nazisti* occupied my village and when I left *Abruzzo*.

It was the look of someone who'd lost hope in the war, and in there being good in the world.

If this war proved anything, it was that there was no more hope to go around. This war had blown it to bits.

If I hadn't gotten out of *Italia*, there was a very good chance that I could have been blown up as well.

Maybe there was one good thing about being here instead of back there.

I hadn't died yet.

Yet.

September 29th, 1943, 6:49am, Falmouth, Cornwall, England

There were homemade jams, toast, a large cardboard box with the words Corn Flakes scrawled on the front, apples, strawberries, and wait, was that... Bacon?

That was supposed to be rationed everywhere.

And then I looked out the small window in the dining room. There was a pig sty not too far away.

Oh.

That was what covered the dining table.

Luca and I just stood in the doorframe, staring at the food, unsure of what to do.

That was a lot of food for breakfast.

Mr. Smithson was reading the paper and Mrs. Smithson was putting jam on her toast before she noticed us standing there like *sciocchi*.

Fools.

"Well, don't just stand there you two, come, sit down,

have some breakfast."

Luca and I exchanged a glance before we stepped into the room and hesitantly sat down at the long table. There were five chairs, one looked out of place, as if it wasn't supposed to be there. It was smaller than the rest, and looked like it had been in an attic somewhere.

I avoided that chair.

It looked as though it could break with a gust of wind.

I looked at all the food.

I didn't know what to do.

What to take.

How to eat it.

Luca, on the other hand, grabbed a piece of bacon and two slices of toast, putting the meat between the bread.

I shrugged, and leaned forward, grabbing an apple and a knife, sliced a small piece and popped it into my mouth, getting rid of any aftertaste of the metallic red liquid from my dream. The crisp taste of the apple made my tongue jump with joy. It'd been a while since I'd had fruit.

"The apples are good, Mrs. Smithson," I said, my accent really showing through with my exhaustion.

I was too tired to hide it. After my interaction with Will I had laid in bed staring at the ceiling, unable to go back to sleep. I was wary I'd have the same dream over and over again.

She smiled, "You think so? We grow them right here in town, there's quite a large garden we all use and tend to, we have to look out for each other, you know."

I nodded, "Of course."

I kept slicing up the apple, leaning back in my chair, perfectly content with listening to Mrs. Smithson go on about the war effort and if everything was going to the troops, there were a few things that they had to keep for themselves. I just inserted words like, "Really?" and "Is that so?" where I felt it was needed.

Then a door slammed from the front of the house, and footsteps started getting closer to the dining room, creaking on the old floorboards.

Blonde hair, blue eyes, pale skin.

Nazista.

"Well, I finished my rounds, Uncle George, and I still got a bunch more papers for the train station today."

Oh. Just, James.

"Excellent, we can leave soon, I just have to finish my breakfast," Mr. Smithson then turned to Luca and I, "If either of you would like to join us at the station, I know James could sure use the company."

I side eyed the blonde.

Eh.

I didn't exactly want to be stuck with the German beauty, but at the same time, I didn't want to be boarded up all day in a house by myself.

I nodded at Mr. Smithson, "I would love to go to the station, it might help me with my English."

He smiled, "Of course Mara, though I think your English is perfect just the way it is."

Except I sounded like a foreigner when I spoke it.

"And what about you Luca?" Mr. Smithson said, looking at me and motioning to Luca.

Oh, right, I was the translator.

I glanced at my best friend, whose hair was still ruffled, he hadn't combed it. A dark shirt that he'd rolled the sleeves up on hung around his upper body, still unbuttoned a few with no undershirt, along with pleated pants.

"Mr. Smithson wants to know if you would like to go to the train station with him and James."

Luca blinked once, and turned to look briefly at James, who averted his gaze towards the ground.

Odd.

"Uh, sure, yes. Are you going?"

I nodded, "I don't want to be cooped up in here one more second, I need to get outside."

Luca chuckled a little, "Of course you do."

I turned back to Mr. Smithson, who, along with his wife, looked incredibly uncomfortable that they couldn't understand what Luca and I were saying.

"He's coming too," I said as I got up, finished with my apple.

"Excellent, just grab some things for lunch, and we'll be good to go."

I tried to translate in my head. Everything went through, except for 'lunch'.

"Uh, *io non capisco* lunch. What is lunch?"

Mrs. Smithson smiled at me, "Mid-day meal."

Oh.

"*Pranzo*," I said to myself.

I watched as James walked over to the table to grab an apple, some strawberries, and a few slices of toast, and put the fruit in one handkerchief and the toast in another, before slipping it into his large satchel full of newspapers.

Mrs. Smithson handed both me and Luca two handkerchiefs and I smiled my thanks, but only grabbed another apple.

I still didn't feel hungry and I doubted I'd be hungry at the train station. Maybe if I didn't eat all day, I'd be hungry enough to eat dinner.

I wrapped the knife I'd been using from before in one cloth, and the apple in another. I almost reached for my pockets, but there were none on my dark green skirt.

The skirt didn't hug me like other skirts that girls my age were wearing. It let me move, and run if I really needed to. A button up white shirt accompanied it, though it was really looking more cream colored these days. The sleeves reached just below my elbows, and the collar was a little wrinkled from being crammed in a suitcase.

Mrs. Smithson smiled, "Oh, I'll get you something to put it in, that way you can drop it off in the ticket booth and won't have to worry about it until lunch."

I smiled, "Thank you."

I excused myself from the table, handing off the apple to her, and running up the stairs into my room, on the excuse that I was freshening up.

When I got to my room, my eyes flew to the dresser, my gun sitting on top of it. I'd taken it out of the pillow this morning thinking I'd be cleaning and polishing it today.

But I wasn't going to. At least not now.

So I grabbed it and placed it under my pillow, back where it belonged.

But as I started to leave there was a voice in the back of my head saying I wasn't going to be safe without it.

I tried to ignore the whisper in my head, but it wouldn't let up. In fact, every step towards the door, it got louder.

I stopped and turned back. Snatching the gun, I slid it in the waistband of my skirt, tucking my shirt in over it so someone couldn't see it.

I ran back down the stairs and smiled at Mr. Smithson, who was waiting at the door with Luca, who passed me a paper bag, and James.

"All ready, Mara?"

"Yes," I said as we started to leave.

The gun burning into my skin as we went.

CHAPTER 6

**September 29th, 1943, 10:34am, Falmouth
Station, Falmouth, Cornwall, England
Mara**

The troops were doing this, the troops were doing that, the troops were going to get shoved up Winston Churchill's *culo* if he didn't shut the hell up.

Couldn't these papers find something else to talk about?

I was sitting on a bench watching the trains come and go, listening to the few people who came by, talking with someone or mumbling to themselves.

Luca was off somewhere learning the ropes of operating the ticket booth from Mr. Smithson, but I wasn't allowed in. Something about how only two people could fit into the booth at a time. Meanwhile, James was suckering any person who walked by into purchasing a paper. He was actually really good at lying.

When he talked about the war, he fantasized. As if the Allies were winning, as if half of London wasn't in ruin, as if half the world wasn't torn up because of one man who wanted power and world domination. It didn't help that I wasn't getting anywhere with the newspaper at the moment. They were using language that I couldn't understand. Military terms I was guessing. That and they were using words that must have been a British thing, words like candor and vigilance and audacity.

I couldn't translate.

I didn't even want to try to figure out what the *fanculo* audacity meant.

They used it a lot to talk about Hitler.

Hitler had the audacity to...

The audacity of Hitler to even suggest...

The one thing they wouldn't say was he was a coward, an imbecile, and a bastard of a man who couldn't even for one second stop to wonder if killing hundreds of thousands of people was a bad idea.

I huffed. I was done trying to translate. I switched the paper to the side that had the comics in it.

Those I could always understand. Besides, they were usually funny.

My newspaper moved.

Not with the wind, but someone was touching it. Bringing it lower and lower, until the flimsy pieces of paper were on my lap.

My eyes snapped to the side, where a boy about my age was sitting right next to me.

His icy blue eyes were sparkling as if they were smiling all on their own.

"I knew I recognised those boots from somewhere."

The voice.

The accent.

My eyes flew up to his hair, black as night, falling down onto his forehead, and pleated pants, a button up shirt exposing an undershirt, and this time, suspenders.

Will.

"Hello, Will." I said with a smile.

He leaned forward a little, inching his way closer to me, "'Ello, *Mara*," he put emphasis on my name, letting it roll off his tongue beautifully.

His icey eyes shifted to the paper, "Comics, heh? I fancy myself a few of 'em every once and awhile. Never pictured you as a comics kind of girl. Are you a comics kind of girl, Mara?" Will asked, raising his eyebrows playfully.

I chuckled, "I might be."

"Always pictured you as a frontpage story girl. Somethin' from the war."

"Already read that, more of the same."

And I couldn't translate half of the stuff it was saying.

Will smirked, "So, Mara, think it's fate? I see you last night, and get the pleasure of seein' you again on this fine mornin'."

I shrugged, "I don't know, Will, maybe it is."

He smiled, and got up from the bench, "Well, maybe the universe is tryin' to tell us somethin'."

"Maybe," I said going back to reading the comics, a woman had just tried to order dinner at eight a.m, "Or, perhaps you're following me?"

Will gasped, "Mara, for you to even suggest that, how dare you disrespect the universe."

A smirk played at my lips, "Oh no, whatever shall I do to make it better?" My voice mechanical and disinterested.

Will chuckled a little, "Well, maybe you could, you know, listen to the universe and take advantage of this."

"Meaning?"

He held out a hand to help me up from the bench but I just stared at it.

"Let's go for a walk."

I raised an eyebrow, "A walk?"

"Yeah, you know, the two of us, together, walkin'."

Don't do it.

Don't do it.

I knew I shouldn't.

We were only in England to get away from trouble, to have boring lives for the rest of the war. I was pretty sure there was some sort of fine print written somewhere about this stating: *NO GOING ON WALKS WITH CHARM-INGLY HANDSOME BOYS.*

Was he?

I mean, the way he carried himself alone could rival any *Italiano* pride, and his smile was spectacular, and the way he was looking at me right now made me want to blush.

But I wouldn't.

Instead, I just looked at the ground for a second, before letting out a huff. Throwing down the newspaper, giving in, I stood up.

Will's smile grew, "Well alright then," he motioned to the far end of the station as if it were an exit or some-thing. It wasn't obvious, the station just stopped, "Right this way."

I nodded as we started walking, hesitant at first.

You have a fottuta gun, you're fine.

Right.

Forgot about that.

Will held out his hand for me to take, which made me look at him, confused.

"Just so you don't get lost."

Right...

"I don't think I have to take your hand to not get lost, Will."

He smirked, "You never know Mara, you never know."

Oh, I did know.

———————

"You seriously 'ave never been to a 'orse race?"

I shook my head, "No, what are they?"

Will laughed, "'Ave you been livin' under a rock or somethin'?"

I smiled, "No, just haven't been out much."

"You've been livin' under a rock, Mara."

"No I haven't."

He sucked in a breath, "You 'ave."

I nudged him a little, "Shut it," I mumbled, smiling as we went.

"What's your favorite color?" he asked.

Ever since we left the station, the questions had just started coming and I actually was enjoying it. We were walking along an abandoned railroad track. Tall grass and wildflowers had mostly covered the rusted metal tracks, and I was trying to balance on them on one side, while Will was trying on the other.

Just two tight-rope walkers getting ready to join the circus.

"Green. Yours?"

"Blue."

"Blue?"

Will turned to me, wobbling a little on the track, "Blue," he then turned back to looking straight ahead, "Alright, my turn, where's the accent from?"

Merda.

I thought I was hiding it better.

"Uh, it's not important."

Will got off the train track, stepping closer to me. We were too close. I jumped off the metal rod and made sure the track was in between us.

"Come on, Mara, it's a beautiful accent, I just wanna

know where it's from."

"I'm sure you don't."

"Yes, I do. Please?" His gaze was intense, it pierced my eyes as if he could read my thoughts.

I took a breath, "Italian."

"What?"

"I'm Italian."

His eyes widened, "Like, Mussolini Italian?"

My fists clenched at the mention of *il duce*, "Yes."

"When did you come over 'ere?"

Lie.

Lie.

You better lie.

But what good would it do? I was a good liar in *Italiana*, but in English, I could never get my voice to sound calm.

"A day ago. They sent us away."

"Who's they?"

I looked at the ground, "*La Resistenza*."

"The Resistance?"

I nodded, "Thought it was safer here."

He let out a low whistle, "Wow."

Silence.

I cleared my throat, "Uh, we should probably start heading back, I don't want to keep my friend waiting, he can't speak English, and you know, it's hard enough as it is and..." I trailed off as I started to walk back towards the station. I knew it was a bad idea as soon as it left my mouth. I knew I shouldn't have said anything. I knew I-

A hand circled around my wrist, pulling me back towards him and I almost collided with his chest with the force. I tried to avert my gaze, paying attention to a peculiar piece of grass over to the left, but a hand came to rest on my shoulder, making my eyes snap up.

Will looked at me, "You're really brave comin' 'ere."

I let out a breath, "I didn't have a damn choice."

"Regardless, I don't think I'll ever know what that kind of war is like, but to me, you're an incredibly brave person for even tryin' to escape."

I blinked, "Thanks."

"And I meant what I said, the accent is beautiful," he said smiling.

I looked up at him, "It's a give away."

"It's mysterious. Last night, I kept askin' myself, 'Who is the mystery girl?' and 'Where, oh where, did she get that gorgeous accent?'"

I laughed a little, "I'm sure you did."

"True story, Mara, I'm tellin' you."

"Okay, I believe you. My turn. Where's your accent from?"

Will smirked at me, "I don't 'ave an accent, where'd you get an idea like that?"

"I have no clue, Will, where would I get that idea?"

He laughed before taking a second to look at me, "You know somethin', Mara? I enjoy talkin' to you."

I raised an eyebrow, "You do?"

"Yeah, I do, and I can't say that about many people."

I stepped back up onto the track, "Neither can I."

I wobbled a little and a hand came around my own to keep me steady.

I glanced over at Will, whose eyes were sparkling, "Well, Mara, seems like we're perfect for each other."

I laughed a little, almost losing my balance as I did.

"Steady," Will muttered under his breath, as his hand flew to the small of my back to keep me from falling, his hand seeming like it was burning into me.

"Don't let me fall, Will," I breathed out. I usually didn't

say things like that, I usually just told people to let go of me. I didn't need saving. But this time, for some reason, I wanted him to keep his hand there.

"Not to worry, I won't."

And I believed him.

For some reason, I found myself trusting him. And I didn't just hand out trust to anyone I met.

I wasn't even sure I trusted my own parents when they were around.

But there was something about how his hand was on the small of my back, how his eyes lit up when I looked at him, and the way his hand gripped mine that made me doubt his words.

I didn't think he could stop me from falling.

September 29th, 1943, 1:25pm, Falmouth, Cornwall, England
Luca

I shouldn't be here.

Mr. Smithson was giving me a lesson on how to sell tickets at the booth. The worst part wasn't being crammed into a small box with a large middle aged man, it was that he expected me to understand what he was saying.

I could get bits and pieces, stuff I could understand from just his actions, but the rest of it made me want to shout.

It was almost as if he forgot I couldn't speak his language.

Mr. Smithson paused for a minute, taking a break from teaching me how to count British money.

It was such a complicated system, sixpence, thru-pence, shillings. Lira was so much easier to understand.

And here, a pound was worth so much. One lira meant nothing, it was half of half of a penny in some respects. But a British pound, that could get a person halfway to Plymouth by train.

Mr. Smithson looked up at the small clock hanging from the wall and his eyes widened, "My God, is that the time? You should get a lunch break, go on then, go eat."

He was speaking too quickly for me to understand, "Uh, *non capisco*, Mr. Smithson."

"Oh, uh, pray-nzo?" he said, mispronouncing something that sounded vaguely familiar. The look on his face though suggested that he believed he was sounding like a native speaker which made me hold in a laugh.

"*Pranzo?*"

"Yes, that's it. Now go have lunch, and tell James as well."

Something about James...

Oh, tell him to eat?

Maybe.

I'd have to pull Mara from her newspaper too. She never ate a lot these days, and it made me worry about her.

I stepped out of the box, but not before grabbing the cloth bag that Mrs. Smithson had put Mara and I's food in.

I found James first, he was standing not too far from the ticket booth, talking to a man about the news I assumed. He kept gesturing towards the front page.

"Sir, are you sure you don't want to hear about what the troops are doing? What the war effort is doing?"

"The war effort can kiss my ass, this thing is taking too damn long."

The man walked away in a huff.

I didn't understand any of it, but James didn't look too happy with the whole thing.

I walked up to him, "Ello," I said, trying to speak English, even though it didn't go beyond just trying.

He smiled at me, "Hiya."

"You, good?" I asked slowly, trying to make the words sound clear.

I knew a few more phrases than I did when we first came here. Mara had tried teaching me a few words on the way to the station today.

James glanced my way, "Could be better. How're you?"

"Uh…"

I hated this. I hated not knowing what to say because I couldn't speak the same language as someone. I hated feeling like I was an idiot.

He laughed a little, putting his hands in his pockets, standing there calmly as I tried to string words together.

"Uh, it is time to eat," I fought to get out.

"Already?"

I nodded, I didn't know what he said, but I just nodded. That's what I'd been doing with Mr. Smithson in the box. Just smile and nod, smile and nod.

I looked around, The bench Mara had been on at the start was vacant.

Odd.

She was probably off punching a wall or shooting a bush or some other form of violence. This whole doing nothing thing must have been torture for her.

I turned back to James, who had taken a seat on the bench that was closest to us. He started to pull out the food from his satchel while I just stood there. I didn't want to sit down if he didn't tell me that I could. What if he just wanted to be alone when he ate?

That would be unlikely, but I wouldn't want to make assumptions that he wanted someone's company. Much less the one person who couldn't speak decent English.

His gaze shifted from his food, to me.

"Don't just stand there, Luca, come sit."

He motioned for me to come towards him, tapping the empty part of the bench to his right.

I smiled a little before going to sit down next to him, putting space in between us.

James eyed the gaping expanse of exposed bench that separated us and chuckled, "I don't bite, you know."

I still didn't understand, but gave a small laugh anyway even though I didn't know why we were laughing.

He grabbed the apple that he had and bit into it. When he pulled away chewing, his lips shone in the afternoon sun.

Why was I looking at his lips?

I mean, they were nice lips, any girl would be lucky to...

Aspetta, cosa?

I shook my head, trying to get myself to come back to my senses. I looked back at him, and James had a smirk on his face.

Did he see me staring?

Merda, what was going on?

James moved his arm with the apple in it towards me, "Apple."

"*Mela.*" I grabbed the red fruit from his hand, and held it up, "Ap-l," I said, butchering the word, but I at least wanted to try.

"*Mela,*" James said. It rolled off his tongue naturally, and I couldn't tell if he was mocking me, or truly trying to pronounce it with the accent. I didn't care either way. It sounded beautiful when he said it.

"*Perfetto*," I breathed out.

He glanced at me, his dark blue eyes paralyzing me, his blonde hair, in a perfect cowlick, had a few strands out of place, and one even fell out onto his forehead. Part of me wanted to brush it out of his face and-

Why the hell would I do that?

I hadn't taken a bite of the apple yet, and I was pretty sure James was going to want it back soon, so I spun it around where it was horizontal and in between my thumb and middle finger, and right where James had taken a bite, I sunk my teeth in right on top of it. I held eye contact with him the whole time, never bothering to blink. I handed the green orb back to James with a small smile.

"Perfect," he translated quietly.

Our eyes never left each other. If only for a second our eyes refused to leave each other. I was lost in the ocean of his eyes, a deep color I'd never even seen before now. My eyes were generic, common, normal, at least by Italian standards. Hazel. That was what most people's eye color was in *Italia.* That or brown. There were a rare few with green eyes, but that was very rare.

I broke eye contact first, choosing to look at the ground instead.

It was a very interesting piece of concrete.

The silence that had formerly not mattered, now engulfed us once again, as only a silence between two people who didn't speak the same language could.

"Bench," James said, creating something other than silence once again.

I turned to look back at him, and he was pointing at the thing we were sitting on.

I smiled, catching onto the game, "*Panchina*."

"Panchina, huh?"

"*Sì.*"

James laughed, and I couldn't help joining in, letting my gaze wander elsewhere around the platform and came to land on Mara walking with a boy.

A boy?

No, that couldn't be right.

But it was.

Mara was walking with a boy. He was taller than her, which wasn't exactly a feat in itself, Mara wasn't the tallest.

I got up from the bench, and James did too, following my gaze.

"Bloody hell, she met Will."

"*Che cosa?*" I asked, looking at him, to which he just smiled a little, laughing to himself.

Mara greeted us with a smile, and the boy she was with, gave both me and James a nod.

"'Ello, James, nice to see you again. And who do we 'ave 'ere?" he said, looking at me.

I didn't know what he was saying and just stared at him blankly.

Mara looked at him, "Will, that's Luca."

Will nodded, and smiled, "Nice to meet you, Luca."

I smiled back, though it was strained, and just nodded my response, unable to figure out the right word for a response.

"I was just showin' Mara around the place, you know, the abandoned train tracks and whatnot," he said, more towards James than me.

"Of course, we wouldn't want Mara to not know about a train track that never gets used, now would we?" James said, his facial expression looked as though he knew something Mara and I didn't.

Will just shrugged.

I turned to my best friend, who was caught up in this English boy, "Mara, *pranza?*"

She snapped out of it, "*Si, andiamo.*"

Yeah, lets go.

She was about to go, but turned back to the boy, "Will I see you around here again?"

He smiled, "Certainly," he said before bowing his head to her, and leaving the station.

Mara was a few steps ahead of us, and I turned to James, who just glanced off after Will.

He shook his head before turning back towards me with a smile, motioning for me to follow him.

But as we were walking, all I could think about was this boy Mara was with. The way she looked at him was a look I recognized all too well.

The last time she looked at a boy like that, he ended up breaking her heart.

James nudged my side, snapping me out of my trance, "You alright?"

I nodded my response as I felt his arm wrap around my shoulders, and I tensed at his touch.

"Come on, don't want to keep Mara waiting."

I nodded once again, unable to think. His arm was around me, and it made my skin surge with some kind of electricity I couldn't place.

Part of me didn't want to place it.

I blinked, shrugging away from him to catch up with Mara, electricity still surging through me.

CHAPTER 7

September 29th, 1943, 7:10pm, Falmouth, Cornwall, England
Mara

"You should have seen him, Hester, give him a few days and he'll be right as rain to work that booth."

"You're forgetting one thing, dear."

"What's that?"

"The boy doesn't speak English."

I smirked.

"Well, he can learn," Mr. Smithson turned his attention towards Luca, "How's about it, Luca, come and work at the train station with me?"

I quickly translated, and Luca looked at Mr. Smithson, "Yes, thank you."

"You're welcome."

'What about me?' I wanted to say, because it didn't seem like he was going to ask me if I could work there. And if I wasn't there, I'd be here with Mrs. Smithson. She was a lovely woman, but I knew what she did while we were gone. She stitched and mended clothing for people around Falmouth, and if I wasn't at the train station, I'd most likely get stuck stitching my days away.

I was okay with work, infact, I needed work. But not that kind of work.

I needed to say something.

We were all at the dinner table having soup of some sort. Chicken stock, carrots, onions, and beef, thrown in a bowl. Supposedly from one of the cows that had been in a field close by.

It was actually fairly good, a lot better than the stuff I'd eaten for dinner back in *la Resistenza*.

I needed to speak up.

I couldn't be cooped up in a house all day. I'd go insane. The restlessness had already settled in as soon as we got back from the station.

"Um, excuse me, Mr. Smithson, if you needed more help, I am sure I could lend a hand."

"Oh, no, I don't suppose there's any more room in the ticket box as is, Mara."

A pause as I tried to gather my thoughts and translate them.

"Oh, uh, not tickets. Uh, I was thinking I could touch up paint, change a few lights, get coal ready for trains. I'm a hard worker and can help with the heavy lifting and repairs."

He chuckled, "Mara, that's very kind of you, and I'm sure you are a very capable young lady in your own right, but I don't think I need someone who's a um-"

"A girl," Mrs. Smithson finished for him, "Besides, a young lady like yourself should be helping to make blankets for the troops, not engaging in rigorous work that would leave any woman severely injured."

I balled my hands into fists under the table, clenching them until I was sure there were going to be welts in my palms. Even the muscles in my jaw were visibly taunt

I blinked and turned to Luca, "She thinks I should be helping make blankets for troops that aren't my own, instead of doing work at the station because I'd be in mortal danger."

Luca snorted, almost choking on the water he was drinking, and looked at me, "Don't rip her heart out, please," he said.

I'd try not to.

I shifted my attention back to the Smithsons, readying myself for the giant revelations I was going to pull out of my *culo.*

Deep breath.

And start.

"Mrs. Smithson, I appreciate the concern for my, um, 'feminine fragility.' However, before the war, I was a farmhand. I worked long hours in the hot sun without breaks or food. I'm a member of the Italian resistance and have seen things that you couldn't even imagine would ever happen. I've opposed my own government, I've clashed with the ENR, I've gotten shot a few times and once had to run with a bullet to the leg and shoot with one in my shoulder. I've pulled bullets out with my fingers and had to bite on a spare shirt to stifle the screams, praying my hands were sterile enough that I wouldn't get an infection. Do not ever question my capability in what you consider to be rigorous work. I will decide what is difficult for myself, and I assure you, lifting a few bags of coal is not anywhere close."

I leaned back in my seat, the gun in my waistband digging into my lower back.

I glanced at Luca who was looking at me with a blank expression, "You tore her apart didn't you?"

I shrugged, "I just assured them I was capable."

"Well, judging by their faces, you did more than just assure them you were capable. I think you scared the *merda* out of them."

"*E stato necessario.*"

It was necessary.

And then, it was dead silent. I looked at James, whose gaze was trained on the floor.

I locked eyes with Mr. Smithson again and smiled, "So, do you think you could give me a chance?" I asked, so calm I wasn't even sure my own *nonna* would recognize my voice.

He cleared his throat, "Well, uh, I lost most of my able workers to the war as it is, so I'm sure I could put you to good use."

Mrs. Smithson whipped her head over to her husband, her gaze narrowed as if she was shooting bullets from her eyes.

I nodded, ignoring her reaction, "Thank you, Mr. Smithson, I appreciate the work." I then turned to his wife, "And ma'am, if I may?"

She stared at me, almost stark white, "Yes, Mara?"

"Thank you. I've done my part in the war already. I don't need to be making blankets for troops who aren't getting sleep as it is."

"That's not true, they're sleeping."

I blinked, "Mrs. Smithson, I speak from a position of experience when I say, they're trying not to get their heads blown off by *Nazisti*. Sleep is the last thing on their mind."

To the side of me, I watched as James coughed up the water he had started to drink, and set it down quickly, before he went back to that piece of tile on the ground.

I snuck a glance back at Mrs. Smithson, who looked as if she might just strangle me. I considered shrinking down and turning into a puddle to escape her stare, but instead, I just smiled at her.

"This is a really nice dinner, Mrs. Smithson, thank you

for cooking," I said, my voice filled with honey.

That did the trick. She didn't say anything, but she did smile to herself, and her face started to return back to its natural color.

Luca nudged me, "What'd you just say?"

"I told her I liked her cooking."

He chuckled a little, "If only it was that easy back home with our parents."

I smiled, "Hey, your parents were alright with us doing stupid *merda*. Mine, not so much."

"True."

I shifted my gaze to James, who was just looking at the two of us, his jaw clenched slightly.

Perhaps it was because he was upset that he couldn't communicate with Luca and I the same way we did with each other. Luca had told me about how James and him couldn't really talk because they couldn't understand each other.

Although, the looks I'd seen them exchange on the way back to the Smithsons house that day made me believe that if they did speak the same language, they'd be close friends.

Luca

"Mara, that was amazing," James said as we all three burst into his room.

I turned to her, "I wish someone could have taken a picture of her face when you started arguing with her," I smiled, talking in Italian.

Mara chuckled a little. Her laugh was deeper and sporadic, layered in with a few snorts if someone really got her laughing. But when she was just chuckling like that, it was light and delicate, and it could make anyone smile. I hadn't seen her laugh like that in a while.

She took a seat on my bed, as if she knew it was mine. She could probably tell by the lack of objects around it. Neither of us brought much more than clothes with us. Though, I was sure I'd seen Mara put her gun in the suitcase. That gun was more than just a piece of metal, it was what she believed had kept her safe during her time with *la Resistenza.*

I sat down next to Mara, and James sat down on his own bed, clearing his throat.

"So is all that stuff true? Everything you said to my Aunt and Uncle?"

She let out a breath, "Yes, it is."

"So you really did get shot?"

I glanced over at her, her face was perfectly calm, but I could feel the blanket grow taunt under my hands as she gripped it. He'd said something about the shooting. Mara loved being in *la Resistenza,* but she never boasted about the shootings she'd been in, or the kinds of places she'd hijacked.

"Yes."

"Wow, that's bloody brilliant."

Mara locked eyes with him.

Merda.

I saw the fire in her eyes as she stared him down, James not even knowing he'd hit a nerve.

"Really? 'Brilliant?' We were caught off guard and I was inexperienced. You don't know what it's like to stare at someone who is from the same country as you, speaks the same language, has the same values of family, and then has to pull that trigger. Brilliant? More like scared and confused."

I looked at her, raising an eyebrow.

"I just called myself scared and confused," she said, speaking in Italian again, her voice low and tired. She must have been exhausted from switching back and forth between languages all day.

"We all were that first day. Remember what I did?"

She snorted, putting her head down for a second, before turning back to James, "Yeah, and this *stupido culo* ran away because he was scared of gunshots."

James laughed.

Wait did she-

Oh mio dio, she told him didn't she?

She definitely did.

That stronzata.

"Mara, did you-"

"Yes."

"You *cazzo*," I cursed before punching her in the arm.

I knew it hurt her, because I saw her face twitch, but she just smirked at me, elbowing my side lightly.

"So how did you two join the Resistance?"

Mara shook her head, "No, you aren't going to ask all the questions. I got some of my own."

James leaned back on the bed, looking amused with her, "Really, like what?"

"Well for starters, why do you live with your aunt and uncle instead of your parents? Did they die?"

I nudged Mara for a translation, and she did.

"You can't just ask that, *idiota*," I said in a low voice, even though I knew James couldn't understand Italian, it felt weird talking right in front of him without lowering my voice ever so slightly.

"Why not?"

"Because it's rude and unsympathetic."

She rolled her eyes, "He asked me about how I got shot, one of the worst experiences of my life. You want to tell me *that's* sympathetic?"

I opened my mouth, and then closed it again.

She did have a point.

I snuck a glance over at James who didn't seem at all phased by the question.

Which meant no, his parents weren't dead.

"You two finished?" he asked.

Mara nodded her response and I flushed a little, realizing he hadn't understood what we were saying.

James cleared his throat, "You know of The Blitz, right?"

Mara once again gave a bob of her head, and then quickly translated for me before he continued.

"Well, I lived in London before the war. And when the day came that the bombs started falling, my mum shipped me out here. Safer that way. And I've been here for the last two years."

Mara blinked, "So your parents could be dead, you just don't know?"

James's face fell and he looked down.

I elbowed Mara, "What the hell did you say?"

She switched to Italian again, "Well, he said he hadn't seen his parents in two years, I just gave him the possibility of them not being alive anymore. Two years *is* a long time to not hear from someone."

I threw my hands up, "You are the most insensitive person I know, you know that?"

She shrugged, "Well, people die these days, Luca. I'm just being realistic."

"Just because it's realistic, Mara, doesn't mean it doesn't hurt a little."

She blinked, her face relaxed, the corners of her mouth tilted downward slightly. Pausing for a second, Mara set herself up to speak in English, before her eyes shifted back over to James.

"Sorry, that wasn't something that I should have said, it's just, when you've been on the verge of civil war for a few years, you learn to try not to care about certain things."

He nodded, "It's okay, Mara. I understand," a smile returned to his face as he looked in between us, "Well, now it's my turn to ask a question. What got you two into the Resistance?"

I saw Mara smile, it was small and paired with how her eyes looked off into the distance wistfully, the gesture came off as sad.

"Well, it's different for each person, everyone has different reasons and different stories. Mine's simple, I was tired of the Fascist government and decided to do something about it instead of sitting around in my house waiting for a raid where a soldier decided to shoot me."

"And Luca?"

"He can talk and I can translate for you." Mara turned to me, "He wants you to tell him how you got into *la Resistenza*."

"Did you tell him your story?"

She nodded, "The short version."

I gave her a smile similar to the one she had when James asked her about her story.

Her short version left a lot of *merda* out.

I glanced at James, who was watching me intently, and smiled at him. I started talking and as I spoke, Mara repeated everything I said in English.

"Um, I guess I have Mara to thank for putting ideas of

freedom and liberty in my head. We'd grown up under the Fascist government, we hadn't known anything else. My parents owned a vineyard, and a lot of what they produced went to the government. We didn't usually have a lot left for ourselves to sell. I got tired of worrying about if we were going to be having pasta for dinner, or bread with olive oil."

I watched as James's gaze turned into one of sympathy.

I took another breath, waiting for Mara to catch up before I started talking again, "And so, I decided, enough was enough, I was done with it. I wanted to be free, like America, or Spain, or England. So, one day, when the ENR soldiers came to our house, I started fighting back, not physically. That's not exactly something I'm good at. I'm good with strategic things, outsmarting people. I slowly dwindled what we gave them. First it was a handful of grapes and olives, and then it was two, and so on and so on. And to me, just that satisfaction of knowing they weren't getting as much from my *famiglia*, was enough to make me smile. But I wanted more than to just take back a few pieces of food. I started wanting to take back what had been freedom to the country twenty years ago. I wanted to know what freedom was like. And so, when Mara said she was conversing with a contact in *Napoli* about the Resistance there, I felt like I had to go."

I shifted my eyes down to my feet, which were nervously bouncing on the wooden floorboards as Mara finished her translation to James. When her voice quieted, I started talking again.

"I left in a hurry. When the letter arrived from *Napoli* we had one day to get there. And my parents, *dio* they were angry. They didn't want me to go get myself killed fighting for a cause that would never win. I told them that was why I needed to fight, because our country needed to have hope. *I* needed to have hope. A year later, and they don't know where I am. They think I'm still in *Napoli*, which judging by what day it is today, I don't think is a good thing," I turned to Mara, who nodded, confirming that *la Resistenza* would be battling it out as we spoke. Or at least we hoped they were still fighting.

"I left my family behind to fight for my country's future, so they can live the rest of their lives free from a fascist power. That's why I joined *la Resistenza*."

The image of my mother, red in the face, tears streaming down her face, yelling at me not to go, while my father physically tried to restrain me from leaving with Mara, played in the back of my mind, and my breath hitched in my throat.

"Papa, you're hurting me, stop. Let me go."

"Is this what you want, to leave your family?" mia madre wailed.

"I need to fight for my country."

"Son, there won't be a country to fight for soon enough," mia padre growled, chiming in.

Then Mara stepped into the house, only to see my father holding me back from the door. I watched as she pulled her gun from the waistband of her pants, holding the weapon out in front of her.

"Mr. Carminico, mi dispiace, but you need to let your son go, this is his choice to make, not yours."

The memory stung.

If I ever got back to Italy, and I for some reason was able to find *mia famiglia* again, I was afraid of what they'd say to me.

I was afraid of what my father would do to me.

He'd kill me for leaving them behind the way I did.

He'd take a piece of farm equipment and run me over with it.

My vision blurred for a second but I blinked away the tears forming in the corners of my eyes. I looked up from the ground, eyes locking with the deep ocean orbs that were trained on me.

Mara cleared her throat as she looked outside the window, the moonlight pouring in, bouncing off the walls.

"Well, it's getting late, I should probably be getting ready in my room to go to sleep. I'll see you both in the morning," she said in Italian and then to James in English.

I nodded at Mara, as a tear slipped down my face.

She saw it, and patted my shoulder, "*Tu bene, fratello?*"

"*Si.*"

"Okay, *buona notte.*"

"*Buona notte.*"

And with that she got up off the bed and left the room, leaving me and James alone.

I blinked again, trying to rid myself of the tears that had formed from thinking about my parents. How the only way I could get out of that house was with Mara holding a gun to my father's leg.

James let out a breath, "Is all that true?"

I laughed a little, "I would make up this?" I said using a little more English. I'd learned a few words by listening to Mara's translations.

He shook his head, "No, no you wouldn't," a pause, "I'm really sorry that happened, I can't even imagine how horrible it was for you there."

If he thought it was bad for me, I wondered what he'd think of Mara's story.

That one was worse than mine.

I shrugged, "I am now here," my accent still kept my

voice from truly getting words out clearly, and my voice wavered a little, but judging by the look on James's face, he could understand.

He nodded, before standing up, and walking over to me, sitting down next to me for a second.

"What are you doing?" I asked wearily.

James's blue eyes locked mine down as his thumb went up to my cheek. I closed my eyes, tensing. Unsure of what he was going to do, and why he was so close.

His thumb brushed against my skin. It was soft, lacking the calluses and cuts I had. He did the same thing again on the other side, and my eyes flickered open. I looked at him confused for a moment. He blinked for a second before nodding. I watched as his hands flew to his face, and he mimed a person crying, before motioning with his finger a path of a tear, and then wiping the invisible trail away.

Oh, he was wiping tears off my face.

He was wiping tears off my face?

A few drops of water escaped, rolling down my cheeks, and James moved his arm closest to me, letting it drape across my shoulders, and leaned me against his side.

"Thank you for telling me about it."

I nodded into his shoulder, and as more memories from home surged through my head, the more tears rolled down my cheeks.

James added another arm, this time on the other side of me, pulling me even closer to him. I could feel his breath fan my neck, and his hands rubbing calming circles on my back.

Was I having a breakdown?

No. I was too calm for a break down.

I might have been having one if I wasn't in James's

arms like this.

This was comforting.

This was safe.

This was nice.

I could stay like this for hours.

And we did, even after I stopped crying James kept holding onto me. At one point, he let go of me, thinking I was asleep because of how still I was, and he leaned me back onto my bed, placing the blanket over me.

"*Buona notte, Luca,*" he had whispered.

And I'd never slept better in my life.

CHAPTER 8

**September 30th, 1943, 3:47pm, Falmouth
Station, Falmouth, Cornwall, England
Mara**

Just a little more to the left.

I inched forward, my arms straining to get the glass bulb into the light hanging high above the ground. Closer and closer.

I was balancing precariously on a rusted metal ladder, trying to change the lightbulbs. They hadn't been changed in a while, and some of them had supposedly been shorting out. And so, I was changing light bulbs in the pouring rain, because I was too stubborn to stop.

Got it.

The lightbulb screwed in and I let out a sigh, balancing myself once again on the ladder before climbing down.

My hair was pulled back in waves that went back to a bun, along with a kerchief that kept the front of my hair from falling in my face.

I was protected from the rain by the awning over my head, but not by much, and when the wind blew, the rain water would curve and move inwards, covering me with a mist.

I grabbed another few lightbulbs from a splintering wooden crate and climbed back up the ladder, the rusted metal creaked and wobbled as I did.

So close. Just a little more.

The ladder was pretty tall, giving me a good five or six feet above the ground, but the lights were spaced out so much that the only way to get to each was by standing on my toes. I knew I could've moved the ladder, I really did, but this was quicker. And I desperately was trying to finish up so I could get out of the rain.

And prove to Mr. Smithson that I could do any of the work he gave me.

Almost.

Almost...

I gritted my teeth in concentration as I tried over and over to get the bulb to stick.

Just a little mo-

The ladder tilted underneath me, and so did I. My leg that was on its toes was unable to stop me from slipping. I flew through the air, my hair loosing itself from the bun and giant strands of it flew into my eyes. My hands flailed to grab onto something that wasn't there and my legs kept waiting to catch on the ground.

I felt light for a second. As if I was just floating. Time seemed to stop as I tumbled, and just for a second, I let out a breath. I felt calm.

And then my body hit concrete.

And that calming breath was knocked out of me.

I heard glass shatter.

My head connected with the ground with a thud, and just when I thought that was it, the ladder came down on top of me, and I heard something crack.

Fanculo, that hurt.

The world spun around me as I laid there, staring up at the sky. The sky that was currently spitting water on my face.

I should probably get up.

I needed to finish replacing the light bulbs.

My hand moved to the back of my head, and though a knot was forming, I felt no blood. I let out a huff, and tried to push myself off the ground, but a burning sensation surged up my leg and split through my torso. I hissed in shock as I felt myself drop back to the ground before I glanced at the mess around me.

The lightbulb I had been holding in my hand was broken into bits, and when I glanced at my leg, I let out a sharp breath. My calf was layered with an even stream of crimson, a large shard of glass sticking straight up from my skin.

Accidenti.

"Mara!" I heard a voice call from somewhere in the distance. I couldn't focus on it though, every time they spoke, it felt like someone took a hammer to my head.

"Mara?"

I let out a grunt in response.

I didn't want whoever it was to think I died.

Too many confessions and tears for me.

I heard someone drop down next to me, rain water sloshing around them. I tilted my head and saw ice blue eyes greeting me as hands gripped the rusty ladder and pulled it off me, my whole body screaming as the pressure was released.

"Mara, are you alright?"

Cockney.

I groaned, "Will, I have a large shard of glass sticking out of my leg. If I was fine, there would be a problem."

He nodded, his eyes filled with concern, "Can you sit up?"

I pushed off the ground again, but snapped back down

when a bolt of pain coursed through my side.

"Hurts," I was able to get out.

Will gripped my hand that I had down by my side, making me relax ever so slightly at the contact.

"Do you think you could fight through it?"

"Why?" I mumbled.

"I know a place that can fix you up, but we gotta be able to walk to it."

I didn't have a choice. It was either lay on the ground surrounded by a puddle of red, or grit my teeth and get help.

Why the fanculo does this hurt more than a bullet?

I nodded, "Okay."

"I'm gonna 'elp you up."

His hold on my hand tightened, and I tilted my head, signalling I was ready.

A searing pain raked up my side as Will helped lift me from the ground. But when my feet steadied themselves on the concrete my leg with the glass in it almost gave out. If it weren't for Will's hands steadying my side I would have collapsed again.

"We need to get that glass out of your leg," he said, almost to himself.

I didn't care if he was referring to when we got to this place he knew or not, I wasn't going to let someone I didn't know pull something from my leg painfully. No, I'd do it myself.

I wobbled a little as I bent down to the hem of my skirt, gripped it in my hands, and ripped it, before taking the piece of cloth and wrapping it around the shard of glass.

"What are you doin'?"

"Taking the piece of glass out," I replied, as if it were obvious.

"Oh, uh, wait, uh, Mara let's not do th-"

I pinched the shard in between my fingers and gritted my teeth as I slowly removed the large piece of glass from my leg. It stung like fire, but I kept going. I had only ever dug bullets out of my skin. Glass was a whole different thing. A bullet had a cylindrical shape, easy to pull, but glass was jagged and bit into the muscle underneath my skin, even as I was easing it out.

Almost there.

I took a deep breath before giving it one last tug, ripping it out.

"*Fanculo,*" I muttered as the gash started to ooze more blood.

I tossed the glass to the side without giving it a second thought and took the cloth in my hand and tied it around my leg, pulling it tight. I grunted at the sharp pain that shot up, but then started to relax a little with the glass gone.

Will looked at me, eyes wide, "You just pulled that out of your leg."

I shrugged, but winced as my side sent a shock wave up me, "Yes?"

"By yourself."

"And?"

He opened his mouth to speak, but then closed it, shaking his head, "Never mind, come on, we gotta get you stitched up and your side checked out."

"My side's fine."

"The guy who's keepin' it from movin' says otherwise."

I huffed, he had a point.

"Okay, let's go."

His grip on me tightened, and we started to slowly leave the station before I stopped.

"Wait, the lights-"

"Mara, you're unable to walk on your own right now and all you can think about is the work?"

"Yes."

Will blinked for a second, "I don't know if I should be concerned, or curious."

"A little bit of both, if we're being honest."

I was surrounded by brick walls and thatched roofs. Dusk had settled on Falmouth and it cast a glow around the cobblestone path we were walking on. The stones were smooth and worn and I was able to slide my leg along them, but every now and then my heel would catch on a cobblestone's edge, and I'd stumble forward.

This part of town was different. Pieces of trash littered the gutters and in some of the homes, the windows were cracked or shattered.

It reminded me of home.

It reminded me of the ENR.

And it made me shiver.

"You cold?" Will asked, looking concerned.

"No, uh, I'm fine thanks."

I tripped on a cobble, making me hiss with pain as my bad leg tried to catch me.

"Careful, we're almost there," Will muttered, his hold on my waist tightened trying to keep me upright.

"Where exactly?"

We turned a corner, and ducked into an alley that had a stench of something dead in it. Will took every step with certainty, nothing to suggest he was lost.

He made his way to an old door rusting on its hinges set into one of the walls and gestured to it with his free hand, "'Ere."

I looked around, "Here?"

"Yeah, come on before anyone sees us."

"What's so bad about-"

His hand circled around my wrist and pulled me into the building. It was colder inside, as if the cold breeze was getting sucked into the house. It was dark, the only light was streaming in through the shattered windows.

There were wooden tables along the walls and next to each was an old nightstand. There was no second floor, it just went straight up to the slanted ceiling. There were lights hanging down from the ceiling which swung back and forth with the cold air coming through the windows.

What the hell was this place?

"Grandpa?" Will called, making the entire space echo with his voice, sending a chill up my spine.

There was no reply, and he sighed, almost in relief.

He moved us over to one of the tables against the wall and slowly lowered me down to sit on it.

"I'll be right back."

I nodded, paying no attention to him. I was more focusing on the blood that was soaking through the cloth tied to my leg, and the searing pain that shot up it.

Will came back a second later with a bag. I watched as he produced a white cloth that he drenched in something from a small bucket on the nightstand next to the table, and pulled up an old wooden stool to sit on. I took the piece of my skirt off the gash, inhaling as I ripped it off some places where the blood was starting to dry. Will started to move the cloth closer to the bloodied mess, but then paused for a second, looking up at me.

"This is gonna 'urt."

I nodded, watching him as he blotted the area.

I ground my teeth together as the pain of the alcohol in gash seared through my leg.

"If it burns, it's workin'."

"So I've been told."

I never got rubbing alcohol. Wine or some sort of whiskey was the closest I had to disinfectant.

Once Will thought the cloth had done its work, he pulled out a spool of thread and a thin needle, trying to thread the silver thing.

On his fourth attempt, I huffed, holding out my hand for him to give me both.

He did.

I licked the end of the thread, and stuck it through the hole in the needle, before tying it off and handing it back to him.

"Where are we?" I asked right before he slid the needle through my skin.

"My grandpa's."

A sharp prick on my skin told me he was sticking the needle through.

I clenched my jaw, but never quite pulled my eyes away from the point digging into my skin and how Will tugged at it so the gash could close up.

"Your grandfather lives here?"

"Oh, uh, no, this is 'is business."

"And what's his business?"

"'E's a volunteer doctor."

"What does- *fanculo*- what does that mean?" I tried to get out through the searing pain that was moving through my leg every time the needle vanished in and out of my skin.

"It means 'e's a doctor for people who can't afford to pay for one. Mostly poor farmers and families who've got someone fightin' in the war."

"Your grandfather's a kind man then."

He nodded, "People do say that about 'im.'" Will's voice was a whisper as he concentrated on closing up the gash.

Three more stitches.

Just three more.

"You alright?"

I nodded.

"You don't 'ave to watch."

"It's better to know what's happening than not."

"Really? A lot of the people my grandfather stitches up don't like to look. They'd rather not know."

I just shrugged in response as he grabbed a couple strips of white cloth from the bag. I held out my hand to do it myself, leaning forward a bit, only for my side to scream in pain.

"*Dio dannazione,*" I cursed, feeling myself pull back to where I was comfortable.

Will looked up at me from where he was sitting, eyes filled with something that might have been concern.

Or pity.

"Where does it 'urt?"

I pointed to my side.

"I'll take a look at it once I get these dressings wrapped around your leg."

"I can do it myself."

"I'm sure you can, but I need to do it in a way that won't pull the stitches."

Any lightness was gone from his voice, instead replaced with a foreign seriousness I hadn't seen from him.

He grabbed my leg, lifting it a little, and started to wrap it in the cotton dressing, layering the material in a way that made me thankful Will was the one who found me.

"I know what I'm doin', Mara."

"I never said you didn't."

"Yes, but offerin' to do somethin' for the doctor isn't the best way to show that you trust 'em."

"You're not a doctor, Will," I said with a smile.

He looked up at me, "Not yet at least."

"You want to be?"

"I want to 'elp people."

"You tried the army?"

He laughed, but it was one filled with a bitter bite to it, "I want to 'elp people. Not kill 'em."

I didn't see the difference.

If you helped someone, you hurt someone. And if you hurt someone, you helped someone. Instead of saying that and speaking my mind, like I did so much it got me in trouble, I just nodded.

"You would make a great doctor."

"Think so?"

"Of course."

If I could get sidelined in the early days of a revolution, anything was possible.

It seemed like he had finished with my leg. He sat up and shifted his attention to my hazel eyes.

"So, your side, is it broken?"

"I don't think so."

"Does it 'urt when you move?"

"Well, I cursed my grandmother's god in a way that could get me slapped in the face, so yes, it does hurt."

"But you aren't cryin' so, probably not broken."

I never cried.

But once again, I bit my tongue. I took my hand and, fighting through the pain, tried to make contact with my ribs. My fingers didn't touch anything out of place.

"Everything feels right."

"Is it bruised?"

I untucked my shirt and lifted it a little to expose a large bluish purple splotch on my olive skin.

Will hissed, "Yeah, that's bruised."

He reached for more cloth strips and when he turned back to me, he paused for a second as if some sort of realization occured.

"I'm gonna need you to uh, well, you know, um..." he trailed off, motioning with his hand towards my shirt.

Oh.

Merda.

"Why?"

"Because, to prevent any more damage to your side, you're gonna need some kind of structure."

"I'll be fine without it, I can walk it off," I huffed.

"You're already causin' bruisin', Mara, if you try to walk it off, you could be in a lot more pain than you're in now."

A pause as that reality settled in.

"So I can't walk it off?" I asked, seeing if that would change the answer.

He shook his head.

I let out a long breath, before shrugging, "Okay, fine."

I reached for my shirt to undo the buttons and Will quickly turned away. I laughed to myself at the rose tint that colored his cheek.

"Are you blushing?"

"No."

Liar.

I slid the shirt off my shoulders and placed it off to the side, wrapping my arms around myself, trying to cover up as much skin as possible before clearing my throat for him to turn around.

When he did, he kept his eyes on the ground as he stepped towards me.

"I'm gonna wrap this around the injury so there's some support as it 'eals. Alright?"

"Yeah."

He got closer, still looking down.

"You're gonna need to look up to see where you're putting the dressings."

He cleared his throat, "Right, you're right," his eyes moved up slowly as he got closer. He held one of the white strips out in front of him as if it was some sort of barrier between us. Will placed it on my side, still not looking directly at me.

The cotton felt weird against my skin and my side screamed with the contact, but that wasn't what I was thinking about. I was thinking about how close Will was. His breath was hitting my exposed shoulder as he worked to wrap the cloth around my torso, and it sent a shiver down my spine.

"You're doin' great," he whispered, as if he couldn't raise his voice any higher.

I bobbed my head in recognition, my mind elsewhere. I focused on every time he'd accidentally touch my skin.

When he'd pull away and apologize, I realized I didn't want him to. I wanted his hands to linger for a second.

More than a second.

And that scared me.

But it also excited me.

I hadn't felt something like this since Marco and I were together. And this, this was fire.

Every brush of skin left a scorching trail, and I really wished he'd just leave his hands on me so I could be set ablaze. Sadly, just as quick as the fire was started, it stopped as he finished the wrapping As soon as he was done, Will jumped back from me, cheeks flaming, making me smirk, that was, before I realized that I didn't have a shirt on, only my *reggiseno.*

I quickly reached for the shirt as he turned away and slipped it back on carefully over the white binding.

"It's just for a few days to offer a little support."

I nodded, "Alright, thank you."

"Yeah, uh, no problem." A pause as we looked at each other for a second, not quite sure whether to address what had just happened or not, "We should probably get you back to the station before Luca and James send out a search party."

I laughed a little, "Luca would never send a search party for me."

"Why's that?"

"I'm always the one having to send one after him. He wouldn't know what the hell to do."

Will smiled, helping me up, the wooden splint digging into my side as I moved. When my feet touched the ground, I stumbled a little, almost falling forward if it wasn't for Will's arm around my waist to steady me.

I nodded my thanks, trying to keep a straight face to hide how fast my heart was still beating.

When we got back to the station I went right back to where I had left off, Luca was still in the booth, but now James was on the other side of the tracks trying his luck with people leaving Falmouth, which I was guessing meant business was slow. The papers were all the same thing anyway. The lightbulbs were still there, but when I tried to move the ladder, my side yelled in protest, and I almost dropped the rusty ladder when I loosened my grip.

"*Merda.*"

"'Ere, let me 'elp," Will said, taking the ladder from me and repositioning it. He reached for a lightbulb and started up the rungs.

"You don't have to-"

"You can't risk pullin' your stitches."

I huffed, "Fine, I'll just sit here and do nothing," I said retreating to a bench close by.

He smirked, "You do that."

After a few minutes of me watching him have a hard time replacing the lights, and some correcting on how he was putting them in, I laughed a little.

"So does this mean I need to be calling you doctor now?"

"Mara..."

"Nevermind," I said, before shifting my eyes to Luca in the booth, who was busy passing tickets to an older couple.

He was getting good at that, just smiling and nodding to people. Probably would be useful later.

My attention then shifted to James, who I noticed had taken a break from selling papers, and instead had shifted his focus elsewhere.

To *mia fratello.*

James

His smile.

Bloody hell his smile.

CHAPTER 9

October 6th, 1943, 11:20am, Falmouth Station, Falmouth, Cornwall, England
Mara

My dark pants were already covered in dirt and coal, and sweat was starting to soak the back of my button up maroon shirt. My side had been hurting less, and the bruise had changed color from an angry blue and purple, to a yellowish brown. I'd hidden it well, re-wrapping my torso every day, tighter and tighter as the pain started to let up.

Luca was working in the ticket booth and I was the one doing the hard work lifting bags of coal, and getting all of it into a large trough. When a train would come I'd be shoveling coal from there.

I was carrying two bags because it was twice as fast and I'd be finished before lunch, which meant I could walk up to Mr. Smithson and ask if there was anything left to do before the trains started moving in. I wanted to see his face when he realized I could do the work twice as fast as others who had worked for him.

Though, the problem with carrying two bags was I couldn't see much of where I was putting my feet, so a lot of it was just hoping to *Dio* that I didn't fall on my ass.

I was so close to the coal bin. Just a few more yards, and then I could race over to Mr. Smithson to gloat. I never bragged unless it was to prove a point, and this was one of those times.

He still didn't think a girl could do what I was doing, and be successful.

And as of that moment, I was very successful in getting the work done.

Anddd... Then my foot caught on a crack in the concrete and I started tumbling forward.

My eyes closed, bracing myself for impact with the hard ground and my arms tightened around the bags of coal I had slung over my shoulder. But I never hit the ground.

Wait, what?

My eyes slowly opened, afraid if I saw I was floating in the air, I'd plummet to the ground in a second.

I looked around and became aware of two arms circled around my waist, keeping me from hitting the concrete. The two coal bags I had been carrying still clutched close to my body.

Who was-

"You gotta be more careful, Mara, I'm not gonna be 'ere every time you fall."

Cockney.

Charming.

Will.

My eyes found him standing beside me with an amused smile on his face. I blinked, his icy eyes somehow warm, but froze me to the spot, waiting for him to say something else.

His arms burned into me almost as much as my gun was. The thought came with the realization that he might have been able to feel the gun in my waistband.

Merda.

I quickly figured out where my feet were, and adjusted to a point where I was upright. In no need of assistance. Although, for some reason, Will's arms lingered around my waist.

I cleared my throat, "You can let go of me now," I said, seeing as I wasn't tumbling towards the ground anymore.

Will nodded, furrowing his brows, "Right, yeah, course, I was just about to do that."

"I'm sure you were."

"I was."

I smiled at him and he did the same, "It's good to see you again, Mara."

"Yes, you too. What are the chances that I'd see you in the same place, at around the exact time I always see you?"

Will smirked, "Oh, unbelievably scarce, Mara, unbelievably scarce."

I loved the way he said my name. It rolled off his tongue perfectly.

"Okay, well, I have to work right now, so, goodbye, Will." I started to walk away, but he caught up to me.

"Wait, Mara 'ey, wait up, 'ow's your side doin'?"

I motioned towards the bags of coal before Will had to grab my arm and pull me to the left to keep me from flipping right over a bench.

"I'm carrying bags of coal, so it's doing good."

"And your leg?"

"Healing over as we speak."

"You take the stitches out?"

I nodded.

With a butter knife that I stole from the kitchen. It hurt like hell, but it was that or have the thread stay in my skin.

"Are you almost done with that?" he gestured towards the coal.

I shrugged, "I don't know. I need to empty the bags for when the next train comes so I don't run out of coal to shovel into the fuel car, and once I'm finished with that, it depends on what Mr. Smithson needs me to do. I already saw the cans of paint in the ticket booth."

Will huffed, "Shame. Thought we could talk again. I really do like talkin' to you."

I nodded, unable to pay attention, talk, and maneuver my way around the station to the coal reserve all at once.

"Look, Mara, do you need 'elp with that?"

"Nope, I'm fine."

"Mara, you can't see. You're gonna get yourself 'urt again. Let me 'elp you."

"Don't need help," I grunted as I almost tripped over another crack.

"Yeah, yeah you do. 'Ere, give me one of those," he said as he grabbed the first coal bag from my shoulders while I tried to mutter some sort of protest. Will sank down a little with the weight of the coal before he got a good grip on it and grunted.

"Bloody 'ell woman, you were carryin' two of these at the same time?"

I shrugged, "I've lifted heavier things."

"Like what?"

"A, um, what's the word? It's what you put on the horses, it turns the fields...Uh, *un aratro*."

My mind was drawing a blank as I tried to sift through the hundreds of words it could possibly be.

"A plow?"

I snapped my fingers as if a lightbulb had just lit up in my head, "Yes, that's the word."

"You lifted a plow, by yourself?"

"Well, I pulled a whole plow by myself, because the horses wouldn't go through mud, and then when it got stuck, yes, I had to lift it myself."

Will stopped dead in his tracks, "My god, are you alright in the 'ead?"

"Probably not," I said with a small laugh.

We'd reached the coal bin, and I lowered the bag to the edge and drove it across the corner so it tore. A cascade of black rock started to shower into the basin, and I had to shake it a few times before it was completely empty.

I motioned to him to hand over the other bag, and he happily gave the heavy thing to me. I did the same thing with this one, my hands already covered in black.

I glanced over at Will, who was watching me intently, like he wanted to ask me something.

"What?"

He shrugged, "Nothin'."

"You look like you want to say something, Will. Just spit it out."

Will huffed, "Well, there's this party happenin' in town tonight."

I raised my eyebrow, "A party?"

"Yeah, you know, music, dancin', that kind of party."

I finished up emptying the bags and threw them into a pile I'd made. Mr. Smithson had told me someone would pick them up later.

"And?" I asked, brushing my hands together, getting rid of any excess coal that could have been taken off before I wiped them on my pants.

"And, I was wonderin' if you'd want to go to an English party?"

I laughed a little, "Me, at a party? With music and dancing?" I looked down at myself, coal covering my clothes and arms, "I don't think so," I said as I started to grab a shovel that was embedded into the bin, starting to turn the coal to get it ready to be shoveled when a train came.

"Oh, come on, it'll be fun, and Luca and James can come too, you all could stand to get out."

I should go.

I should say yes.

This was a way to make the most of the situation at hand.

But I didn't think it would be the best idea for me to go to a party with a bunch of people all packed together. I could say something or do something that wasn't okay. And mentally, I didn't think I was ready to be with a large crowd of people.

I was carrying a gun on my waist so I could feel safe.

A crowd of people was not going to help my feeling of safety.

But if Luca was there, maybe that would be better. He'd be there for me.

"Luca and James can go?"

Will smirked. He could tell I was starting to give in, "Yes."

"And you'll be there?'

"Yes."

I huffed, "Well, then I guess I could try to..." I trailed off, the word that I was looking for refused to translate into English.

"Go to a party?"

"Yeah, that."

Will's smirk changed into a large smile, and then a panicked expression crossed his face, as if he hadn't planned this far ahead into the conversation, "Great, uh, well, I, erm, actually 'ave to go, I just wanted to pop in and see you, uh, but that's great, that's amazin', uh, I'll see you then?"

I nodded as he started to walk backwards away from me, "Yes, you will."

"Good, okay, goodbye, Mara."

"Goodbye, Will."

As he ran off, I couldn't stop myself from smiling. I felt like I was floating for a second. But then that feeling of being light on my feet gave way to a weight that pulled me back down.

What the hell was I going to wear? How was I going to get there? How the hell was I going to convince Luca and James to go?

So much for being happy.

Being anxious was so much easier.

"No."

"*Perfavore, Luca?*"

"No."

"But-"

"Mara, I'm not going to some British party with you and a guy."

"Luca, I need you there."

"Why? So you can ditch me? I don't know if you remember this, but we've been in this situation before, before *la Resistenza* with Marco and you."

"I don't know what you're talking about," I said, averting my eyes away from him.

"Uh, yes you do, you ditched me, sitting by myself, so you could run off with him. Tonight's going to be no different."

"Luca, it's not like that with-"

"Can someone please tell me what the bloody hell you two are arguing about?"

Oh.

Right.

Forgot James was there.

I looked over at him, "I'm trying to convince Luca to come to this party that Will wants me to go to. You can come too if you'd like."

James blinked for a moment, shifting his attention from me, to Luca standing next to me, "If I'm being honest, I'd love to get the bloody hell out of this house for once."

I turned to Luca, switching back to Italian, "James is going."

"Really, Mara? You think I'm going to go just because James is going?"

"No, I think you're going to go because you don't want to be left alone with Mrs. Smithson and her blankets."

Luca's eyes widened, before clearing his throat, "Okay, so when is the party?"

"Tonight, in town supposedly," I said before I looked at James and told him the same thing in English.

The blonde nodded, "Right, so that means we should all start getting ready if we want to trick Aunt Hester into letting us go. We just got to be all dressed up and ready so she doesn't want all the effort to go to waste."

I raised an eyebrow, "You sound like you've done this before."

"I have."

"Well, then, I'm all ready to go," I said, gesturing to my work pants and shirt, which made James laugh.

"You can't wear that to a swing party."

"Why?"

"Girls wear dresses. You know, dress up and all, try to grab people's attention."

I scoffed, "But I don't *want* to grab people's attention."

"Mara, if you go in that, they will be paying attention to you."

He had a point. I had a better chance of blending in with a dress, than the dirty pants and shirt I was wearing.

I let out a breath, "Fine. What about Luca?"

"I'll help him."

I nodded and glanced at my friend.

"He's going to help you get ready, supposedly people want to be noticed at these things."

The ones in Italy were more come as you were, no one really cared because sometimes all people had was what they had worn to work.

Luca looked at me, "Why would someone want to be noticed? It's dancing."

I smiled, "That's what I said."

He smirked, "Well, you should go start getting ready, it's already five."

Damn it.

"Yeah, I will."

"So, go get dressed, you have to stand out, right?"

"Trust me, I don't think I'll have a hard time doing that."

He smiled, "Me neither."

I gave a small smile before I headed over to my room to get ready.

I didn't understand why people wanted to stand out. Standing out meant you got noticed, and where I came from, being noticed wasn't a good thing. Especially with a bunch of ENR soldiers lurking around town.

Standing out meant you had a target on your back. And I didn't think I wanted that here.

_____

James

I was fixing my hair in the mirror with a comb, trying to get just the right amount of wave, slicking back the one side that was short. Pomade was already in my hair, it was just a matter of *how* I used the stuff. I hadn't bothered to button up my shirt yet and it hung loosely off my shoulders.

I glanced over at Luca, who'd supposedly been ready for a while now.

The same shirt he had been wearing from before, still only buttoned half way.

The girls would love that.

His hair was a mess though. There wasn't any product in it, and it went one way or the other, a few strands falling into his eyes.

He wasn't ready.

I finished doing my hair and grabbed the Pomade, tossing the bottle to Luca.

He caught it, but looked at it for a second trying to recognise what it was, and when he seemed to get it, he shook his head.

"No."

"What do you mean no? You look like some sort of hoodlum."

I got a raised eyebrow.

Oh, right.

I walked up to him and ficked a piece of his hair, making a thumbs down sign in order to tell him about his poor choice in hairstyle.

Luca laughed a little, before handing me back the container, "I don't need."

I threw my hands up. If he wanted his hair to look like a mess, he could be my guest.

I put the jar back on my dresser before starting to straighten out my shirt and button it up.

My eyes shifted over to Luca once again. We locked eyes and he quickly turned away, his cheeks red. I glanced at him as he got up from the bed and went over to the mirror, looking at his hair. He ran a hand through it twice before letting it be.

I noticed that his shirt was wrinkled, and in some places, had dirt on it.

Or was it blood?

It was red.

Definitely blood.

Did I want to know why he had blood on his shirt?

No.

But did I want him walking into a party with blood on his shirt?

Absolutely not.

I walked past him to my closet off to the side, and pulled out a white button up.

"Here," I said, handing him the piece of clothing.

He looked at it for a second, confused, before I pointed at the blood stain on his shirt. He looked surprised that it was there, before a wave of understanding crossed his face.

"Mara," Luca muttered, shaking his head, "*Le ho detto di non toccare.*"

Something about not touching?

Maybe she shouldn't have touched it?

Why did she use his shirt?

Why had she been bleeding?

I shook off my questions as he took the shirt and started unbuttoning his own.

I turned away, deciding to go try to read a few sentences of *Cannery Row* before we had to leave.

What the bloody hell was this hallucinating lunatic talking about?

As I kept reading, I felt my gaze flicker over to Luca every once and awhile. He was in the middle of trying to figure out which way was right side out on the shirt. But that wasn't what I was focused on, the thing that I should have been laughing at because he had a lapse in memory and had forgotten how to put on a shirt. No, my eyes were drawn to his shoulder blades, and how his back was perfectly toned, and how when he turned a little, I could see his exposed chest.

I blinked once, and then again.

What the hell was wrong with me?

It was John Steinback.

The lunatic had me thinking about a word and a thing, and my brain was a muddled mess already.

Perhaps if I kept reading...

Yeah, that would do it. And it'd get me to stop looking at Luca.

My eyes darted across the page once again.

How can a word...

No, nope, don't think about it, it's American literature, it's going to sound a little crazy.

I mean, The Adventures of Tom Sawyer?

I'd never been so unabashedly confused in my life.

But now?

I think this was worse.

My gaze once again shifted over to the Italian only a

few feet away from me, who was just finishing up buttoning the shirt. Once again, only to the fifth button.

What was it with him and not buttoning shirts?

He had rolled up the sleeves to where they ended at his elbow, and part of the shirt was tucked in, the other part was hanging loosely out.

On one hand he looked like a drunk coming home from a long night at the pub. On the other, he looked, in his own way, great.

He looked great.

I nodded when he turned towards me and gave him a thumbs up.

He looked me up and down, and then returned the gesture, making me smile.

"*Di bell'aspetto,*" Luca said, almost to himself.

"Who is?" An accented voice asked from the doorway, making me jump a little before turning to see Mara, standing there in an emerald dress.

It looked lightweight and hugged her waist before dropping freely down to her knees. The sleeves only went down about halfway from her shoulder to her elbow, and the neckline gave a v-shape. Up at the top, there were pieces of fabric that suggested some sort of shrug was sewn onto it to cover the shoulders completely. Her shoes weren't the same boots as I'd seen her wear since she got here, they were different. Strappy leather heels, with a buckled strap going across the ankle to keep them in place. They looked worn, as if they could break at any second. The brass buckle looked like it was going to fall off, but was held on by a few scraps of thread that had been added to it.

Her hair was as it always was, the sides pinned, and the rest fell to her shoulders, but she'd brushed it out, making it look a little more put together.

She looked beautiful.

"It's not polite to stare, both of you," she said with a smirk, which made me look away, clearing my throat.

She turned to Luca, "*Chi e?*"

I recognized the word, I'd heard it before in my classes in London.

Who is?

Luca paused for a second before shrugging, "*Mi.*"

Mara laughed, "Of course it is. Anyway, you two ready to make Mrs. Smithson let us go?"

I smiled, "Mara, we're not *making* her do anything. Aunt Hester can say no if she really wants to. But if we really do want to get out of here we should start to leave now. Especially if we don't want to be late."

She blinked, "We don't even know the time, Will never said."

"He didn't have to. Parties around here start when the sun goes down," I glanced out the window to see the sky turning from red to dark purple, "And judging by the sky, we need to be quick if we want to get there in time."

Mara translated for Luca, who nodded and started for the door. He glanced at me as we went with a small smile on his face. His eyes went from my shoes to almost my eyes, and I felt myself shiver a little at the way his green and brown mess of eyes were gazing at me.

And the worst part was I didn't hate the feeling looking in his eyes gave me.

CHAPTER 10

October 6th, 1943, 8:01pm, Falmouth, Cornwall, England
Mara

The crisp air pricked my exposed skin. With the sun down, it was colder, and I hadn't been this exposed in a while.

It wasn't dreadful.

I'd been in worse conditions, but I usually was wearing more than what I had on.

James and Luca had gone into the large one story metal box I was standing in front of already, leaving me outside hoping Will wasn't already in there. James had said if he had been there, he would've waited outside for us.

So I was standing outside, waiting for a guy.

The music inside played in my ear, a deeper male voice paired with two women, who were singing about a Pistol Packin' Mama.

I didn't get it.

I gazed up at the stars painting the night sky and took in a deep breath.

Maybe I should just go in?

Yeah, it was too cold outside anyway.

And just as I was about to turn on my heels, my actual two inch heels, which were a real pain in the *culo* to walk in, I heard a familiar voice call out.

"Mara, is that you?"

I tried to figure out where it was coming from, and my eyes locked with Will, who was standing a few paces off from me.

His hair wasn't slick back like I'd seen a lot of the men doing, it was how it had looked the last few times I'd seen him. It still had the same shine as the others, but those few strands were still draped over his forehead.

"Will?" I asked, just to be sure.

"That'd be me."

He got closer, and his smile grew as he saw me in the light of the building's open door.

"Damn, you look beautiful," Will said as he took my hand, "The other guys are gonna be so jealous I got a girl like you with me."

He twirled me, bringing our hands up over my head, my skirt flying out as I turned. I couldn't help laughing a little as I spun. His hand never let go of mine, even when we stopped.

"You don't look too bad yourself," I smiled as I glanced at what he was wearing.

Dark pants, a creme shirt, and a greyish-black tweed coat, unbuttoned. He looked nice.

Handsome.

He looked handsome.

Attractive.

There was no doubt about it, ever since I saw him on the beach.

He was definitely attractive.

Maybe it was the combination of features I had only heard about in books. The icy blue eyes, the black hair, and the pale skin I'd never seen put together.

But that combination was standing right in front of

me, and the result was simply, well, charming to say the least.

"Why thank you. We should probably go in though, wouldn't want you to catch a cold out 'ere."

I laughed a little, "Believe me, catching a cold is the last thing on my mind right now."

He smiled, "Well, what is?"

Oh, well lets see, there's the constant fear I'm going to be killed at any second.

The scary truth the Axis Powers might win the war and Italy might never be free.

The thought that I had friends in *la Resistenza* who were risking their lives at the moment and half of them could be dead.

So a few things.

I could have said all that.

But for fear of being sent to a doctor about my thoughts I just smiled and said, "Dancing."

Will burst out laughing, "Dancin'?"

"I can't dance."

"Everyone can dance."

"Everyone except me."

He blinked, "I don't think that's true."

"Really?"

"Really. In fact, when we get in there, we're goin' straight to the dance floor, and I'm gonna teach you 'ow to dance."

"I don't think that's a good idea."

"On the contrary, Mara, I think it's an excellent idea."

"You might be saying something different when I keep stepping on your toe."

"We'll find out, won't we?"

Will gripped my hand tighter and guided me into the

building.

It was bright, everything was lit up with large lights, some hanging down from the ceiling in mismatched order, others were floor lamps, standing in the corners and on the outskirts of the dance floor.

The music was louder in here and my senses were overwhelmed with the smell of cheap alcohol and tobacco, as well as all the people around me, talking, laughing, dancing. Part of me wanted to curl up in a ball and disappear from this place. The other part wanted to run straight into the middle of it.

I had no time to decide which part of me won, as Will dragged me onto the dance floor.

And then we were in the middle, with everyone else.

I just stood there, I had no idea what to do. But Will's hand was still holding mine, and it made me feel a little safer.

He spun me around before pulling me into him, his other hand grabbed my free one.

"And now, we Swing."

"Swing?"

He straightened his arms slowly, giving distance in between us, and then pulled me back in, and slowly repeated the process again. I stumbled a little over my own feet, trying to remember when to pull away and when to get pulled in.

He let go of one of my hands, taking me to the side, before twirling me into his arms.

We did that a couple more times.

"And that, Mara, is Swing. Faster?"

"That was slow?"

Will stifled a laugh, "Come on, try it."

I huffed, "Fine."

And we sped up. I was spinning, moving back and forth and side to side. Wait, was I-

"You're gettin' it now," Will said, looking at me encouragingly.

I couldn't help a small smile from playing at my lips, "*Merda,* I'm actually dancing."

"Yes, yes you are."

And then the song changed.

This one wasn't as fast and upbeat.

It was slower.

"Frank Sinatra," Will said, his voice quieter.

"Who?"

"'E's a famous singer from America."

"Oh. I don't know who that is."

Will smiled, "Well, we might just 'ave to change that. See, this song, it's called *The Song is You,* good isn't it?"

I nodded my response as one of his hands let go of mine, and went to wrap around my waist. He used his free hand to position one of my hands on his shoulder and held the other in his hand.

"Now what?" I asked.

"Now, this is the best kind of dance, you don't 'ave to do anythin'."

I raised an eyebrow, "Really?"

"Yeah, all you gotta do is just rock back and forth."

He started swaying us from the right to the left.

"Back and forth?"

"Yeah, back and forth."

"And that's it?"

Will looked down at me, "That's it."

So we rocked back and forth, staring at each other.

Dead silence.

But the way he was looking at me in that moment, was

doing all the talking.

The way he was looking at me made me feel like I was the only one in the room.

I hadn't gotten that look in a while.

When the song ended after what seemed like an hour, yet another faster 'Swing' song came on. Will blinked, something that I couldn't remember if he'd done during the dance.

Come to think of it, had I blinked?

That wasn't important.

"You want to get some air? It's a little stuffy in 'ere."

I looked around and once again became aware of all the people around me. The noise, the smoke, the smell, how boxed in I felt. It looked like everyone was closing in on me, and I could feel my heart start to race, my breath labored as I tried to get it out. My eyes darted around the room, starting to panic.

I was going to start having an attack if I didn't get out of the building.

I nodded and tried not to seem like I was escaping as we walked out the door.

I was forgetting something.

Oh, *merda.* I forgot about Luca.

Again.

I stopped for a second, "Wait, what about Luca and James?"

Will waved it off, "They're fine, probably dancin' or talkin' to some girls."

"But Luca, he can't speak English. I mean, I've been teaching him some words and sentences, but he can't-"

"Mara, 'e'll be fine, James is there with 'im, and I can guarantee 'e's not gonna let anythin' 'appen to your friend."

He was right, James would watch out for him. At least, he better, or I was going to shoot him in the foot.

"Now, come on, let's get the 'ell out of this place."

Luca

He was talking to some red-head. She was smiling, he was smiling, and I was sitting off to the side watching with my hands in my pockets like some dumbass who didn't know how to talk to girls.

I was the one every girl wanted back in *Italia*.

A smile could get me five dances.

Now?

My smile was all I had, if a girl started talking to me here, I'd just have to blink and tell her in *very* broken English that I didn't understand her.

Mara had taught me a few more phrases on my way to the dance, along with some random extra words. Telling someone I couldn't understand a word they were saying was one of the phrases I'd been repeating in my head again and again.

I kept watching James with the girl, talking to her.

But then, when she gestured to the dance floor, he shook his head. They exchanged a couple more smiles before James turned towards me and headed my way.

"You look rough," he said with a smile.

Did I really look that miserable?

I motioned towards everything around us, before pointing at myself and shaking my head.

"This isn't your thing?"

"Not in England."

James laughed a little.

"Why don't dance with her?" I asked, knowing that

my pronunciation was *merda* and my words didn't make sense.

"Eh, not really my type." His eyes locked with mine, before they darted up and down my frame. Just the way he was looking at me made me want to vanish into thin air. I didn't know why and I didn't know what the look meant. All I knew was he was looking at me in a way no man should be looking at another man. It made my stomach twist, but oddly, not in a bad way.

It wasn't *farfalle,* butterflies, like Mara had described to me when she first started to talk about Marco in the way a girl does once she starts to take interest in someone.

While it was funny to hear Mara all giddy, that wasn't what I was feeling. This was different. It was, well, twisting my stomach.

I couldn't figure out what was going on. Not over the music, not over the people.

So I said something that Mara had taught me to say, "You want to get out of here?"

I was supposed to say that when I met a nice girl and didn't want to be under the watchful gaze of a whole town. But I'd just said it to James.

And it wasn't just to get out from under the town's eye, it was to truly just get out of the building. The walls were starting to close in, and if they had started closing in for me, Mara was already long gone. Her fear of small spaces went well beyond mine.

James was quiet for a moment, which made me start to question if I had said the right thing.

Dio, I really hoped I didn't end up saying something that actually meant, 'You're shit.'

But then he smiled, and nodded, "Yeah, I'd like that."

That was one of the phrases Mara had taught me as we

walked here, saying it was one of the responses.

We started to move around people, away from the music and the crowds, and when we got outside, the fresh air greeted both of us.

And then it hit me.

Merda santa, he knew that was the line Mara gave me to ask girls to get out of there.

Kill me.

Please, kill me now.

Mara

The cobblestone gripped at my bare feet, my hand holding onto my shoes.

These shoes would barely stand a chance on cobblestone.

Will was next to me, and all I could think about was my free hand intertwined with his.

We'd been walking around the town and he was showing me a few of his favorite spots. The bakery, where they'd make pies, and the fruit stand where strawberries and apples were in high demand. The liquor store, which was his personal favorite, he'd stolen a bottle of whiskey from it once, still had the thing as a trophy. Never got around to drinking it.

"So, when would you drink it?"

He shrugged, "I dunno, maybe when the war's over."

I smiled sadly, "I think you mean, *if* the war's ever over. When you've seen what I've seen you start to believe war is an endless cycle."

He nodded, as we reached a square sort of place, where there were park benches, and trees planted. He motioned for us to sit down and when we did, he gripped my hand a little tighter.

"Why do you say that? What 'appened back in Italy, Mara? What exactly did you see?"

I bit my lip, shivering. Not from the question, but from a gust of wind that had blown my way. The cool air had been fine, but we were getting closer to the ocean, as made evident by the sea gulls flying above us, and the faint smell of salt my nose kept getting hints of every time the wind blew.

Without a word, Will took off his coat, and started to drape it over my shoulders. I tried to shrug him off.

"Mara, take the coat."

"I don't need the coat."

A hand flew to my cheek.

His hands were warm.

"Mara, you're freezin'."

"I hadn't noticed."

"Mara, I'm goin' to put this jacket over you and you're not goin' to refuse."

"Why?"

"Because I'm bein' a gentleman, tryin' to keep a woman warm."

And because my stubborn *culo* couldn't sit there and let him say that *he* had to keep me warm, I protested, once again pushing away the coat.

"I'm perfectly capable of keeping myself warm."

"Mara, you're gonna catch a cold."

I shrugged, "Wouldn't be the worst thing that's happened to me."

"Well, I don't care, I care that you don't get 'ypothermia and die from the cold, so put the damn jacket on."

I raised an eyebrow.

He huffed, "Please?"

"*Per favore.*"

"Huh?"

"Please. It means please."

Will smirked, "Well then, *Mara,* would you be so kind to put on the jacket so you don't die from the cold, *per favore,*" he exaggerated the please, making it sound like a dramatic opera, which made me laugh, my stubbornness fading away.

"Fine."

I felt the warmth of the coat start to drop down on my shoulders, and I wrapped it around my frame. I hadn't realized how cold I was until the jacket started to thaw my arms. As I inhaled the crisp air, my nose caught the smell of the coat: tobacco and burnt wood. It was a smell that made me feel safe.

"So, tell me about Italy."

I blinked, "What do you want to know?"

"I want to understand, Mara. I want to know about what 'appened back there that made you who you are."

I smiled, "Well then, I suppose I should start at the beginning. I was born in Abruzzo, a small region of Italy, under Mussolini's government. I haven't known a world where I didn't live in a fascist society, where I was scared a raid would happen one day, and change everything. Luca and I were practically raised together. But I was always the problem. I always got into fights, said things at school that a girl shouldn't say-"

"What? You?" Will said with a smirk.

"I know, who would have thought? Luca's parents didn't exactly like me, but they never complained about their son having a friend, and a friend who was willing to do farm work without pay. They owned a vineyard, most of it went to the government though. I helped them a lot with it. I lived in a bubble for the first ten or eleven years of my life. But then I started to notice the world, and how we as a country lived. I became invested in freedom, something that was whispered about amongst the old men who stood outside churches on Sundays waiting for their wives to finish talking with *Dio.*

"I loved the word. Freedom. I loved the way it sounded, everything about it. I dreamt of it. I pulled Luca and another good friend into my daydreams. And then, there was an accident. There were several raids that happened on the same day. They all went horribly wrong. People died, good people, gone. And so that was when I knew I had to act. I got Luca to do it too, to go and fight. And my other friend, well, he betrayed us all when he went to *Roma*, and enlisted in the ENR. But Luca and I made our way to *Napoli*, where we'd heard a resistance presence was moving in. I have always said everyone has their own story of why they joined *la Resistenza.* Luca joined because the ENR took so much from his family there was barely enough food to sell or eat and he was tired of it. I joined because I saw my family bleed out in front of me with bullets lodged into them, from guns that were supposed to protect them from harm."

I paused for a second, looking at Will, seeing if I should shut up yet. His eyes, though almost unseeable in the moonlight, were still there, and they encouraged me to continue.

I took a deep breath.

"I needed to stand up for something because I needed to know there was a way to stop innocent people from getting murdered by their own country. I needed hope. And when I joined *la Resistenza*, I finally started to find hope. I'd learned to shoot a gun from my father, who had said that a girl always needed to know how to use a gun, in case the man in the house was gone. So, I was one of the field operators at the start, because if things got rough, I knew how to defend myself. I started out going on supply runs. Took things like bandages, food, water, ammunition. But then around my second week, we were ambushed, I took a few hits, and my entire perspective changed.

"I wasn't just fighting for something any more, I was fighting against something. I started doing harder runs, hits on ENR posts, small shoot outs. I got to the point where I was planning hit and runs. But then, we started getting organized, preparing for something. That's when *la Resistenza* and all its branches decided it was safer if the younger members were sent away to safe houses. Which brought me here," I stated with a small smile.

There was a pause for a brief moment before Will decided to speak.

"You were *in* the Resistance?"

I nodded.

"Like the one that's fightin' right now in the Civil War?"

Another nod.

Will turned to face me, "Mara, you realize 'ow brave that is, right?"

"You've said that before."

"Yeah, well that was when I thought you were just bein' 'elped by the Resistance. Didn't think you were actually in it."

I let out a breath, "It might be brave, but the trade off is seeing things no one should have to see, to be forced to make the sacrifice of one person dying, to save many. And it might sound like a simple decision, until it's yours to make."

His hands went to my shoulders, holding me up, "And that makes you braver than most people in this world."

My eyes locked with his, the icy stare petrifying me again.

I shook my head, "I don't think I'm brave."

"Why not?"

"Brave would be staying and fighting, not fleeing to a safe house. That's cowardly."

Will smiled, a hand coming up to cup my cheek, "Cowardly is standin' by and doin' nothin'. Mara, you witnessed people you cared about dyin', and even so, you went to Naples to 'elp. You bounced right back up even after everythin'."

But at what cost?

I wasn't going to lie, I knew I had flashbacks.

I knew I had triggers.

I knew I had symptoms of shell-shock.

I didn't bounce back up.

I started falling down a long staircase, and I still was.

I wanted to correct Will, tell him I had a gun on a belt I had placed under my dress because I was still afraid someone was going to kill me.

I wasn't bouncing back.

I knew it.

But no one else did.

Not even Luca knew the extent of what I was going through.

The panic attacks, we both had. Different things set us off, but still had the same effect.

But he'd never actually experienced the things I had. He hadn't had to kill anyone.

And I was very glad he didn't.

Two damaged people was enough.

Two damaged people who had flashbacks and nightmares about dying, and killing and the people they've killed. Who are always looking over their shoulder...

That would be too much.

I bit my tongue.

Will didn't need to know.

He didn't need to know about the nightmares, the gun, the panics, the shell-shock, the trust issues, the detachment issues, the not feeling certain emotions because I'd learned to ignore them.

"You're brilliant Mara, and those things you did, don't make you any less brilliant, they make you brave and strong. You're a strong person, Mara, I admire that in you."

"You do?"

Will smirked, "Yes, Mara. Is that so hard to believe?"

His thumb stroked my cheek, and his eyes darted between mine, and lower on my face. My lips. I felt him start to lean in closer, and closer, and closer, until his lips grazed mine. But they didn't touch yet.

"I'd like to kiss you now, if that's alright?"

I pulled back a little, "You have to ask?"

"Well, I don't know if you've got some 'andsome Italian guy back in Italy waitin' for you or not."

I laughed, "No, I don't have someone back home."

"Oh thank the Lord," He breathed out, before his hand cupped my face tighter, and pulled me into him, pressing his lips to mine.

The kiss made time stop. As if everything else around us disappeared. The buildings, the trees, the seagulls cawing at us for having the audacity to be anywhere near them. It was just me, and him, together.

And that both excited and terrified me.

But in that moment, in the second after he had first started kissing me, in that instance when I decided to kiss back, I made a decision.

He didn't need to know I was broken.

Because from where I stood, he thought I was brave and strong, and if I told him the whole truth, I wouldn't be brave and strong.

I'd be broken and bruised.

And he might have liked that I was strong, but he wasn't going to like that I was damaged.

Because if someone was broken, you couldn't put them back together as easily as you could put together a plate with some glue.

It took years for you to even find the right stuff to use.

CHAPTER 11

October 7th, 1943, 11:23pm, Falmouth,
Cornwall, England
James

His eyes were filled with amazement as he glanced at the sky.

"*Che Bella*," he breathed out.

I raised an eyebrow, "You haven't seen the stars before?"

Luca and I were in a field, tucked behind a hay bail. We were sitting down against the bale, the wet grass soaking into our pants. Our eyes trained on the night sky.

His stare shifted from the clear sky, to me, and he smiled.

"I have. Not in England."

I nodded.

Silence engulfed us once again. I wondered what we would say to each other if we could speak the same language. If we'd still be stuck in silence, because it felt like I needed to know so much about him.

I wanted to know his favorite color, his favorite animal, his favorite food, all the things that seemed top priority when I was a kid trying to get to know someone. Then there were the deeper questions that had become topics of discussion nowadays when meeting someone.

What do you suppose you'll do once the war's over?

Yeah. That question.

I didn't know what I'd do. I doubted Luca knew what he'd do either.

I watched as he picked at the grass beside him, and I smiled a little at how fidgety he was. He glanced over, and our eyes met.

He smiled at me, "You didn't have to leave. I saw girls want to dance with you."

I blinked, "I didn't want to dance with any of them."

"Why?"

I shrugged, "Not my type."

He scoffed a little, "What is, then?"

"I dunno," I said, almost as a whisper, looking back up at the stars.

And that was the truth. In London, I was just turning the age where I started to notice girls, but I had to leave before I had the chance to really develop feelings for anyone. Sure, when I came to Falmouth, there were a handful of girls who all wanted to dance with the boy from London. But I'd never taken a liking to any of them. In fact, I'd never actually felt what it was like to fancy someone.

"I think I might be broken," I said, thinking out loud.

"*Che cosa?*" Luca asked in confusion.

I pointed at myself and then grabbed a piece of hay, breaking it in the middle, "Broken."

"*Rotto?*" Luca laughed a little, "You are not *rotto*. You have not found someone to dance with."

I blinked, looking at him through the tops of my eyelids, "Maybe."

The worst part was, I had wanted to dance with someone.

They'd been standing off to the side, watching me turn away girl after girl.

But I couldn't.

Boys didn't dance with boys, unless it was as a joke. I wanted to dance with Luca, but not as a joke.

I loved the way he squirmed when I was looking at him. As if I could drown him if he locked eyes with me.

"Luca?"

"Hmm?"

His hazel eyes hesitantly shifted away from the ground, and he froze when they met my stare. It was as if he got lost. I was doing quite a bit of getting lost myself. I was fixated on the flecks of brown in a circle of green, and sometimes flecks of green in a circle of brown. I couldn't tell which it was.

You going to say anything, or just keep staring?

Oh, right.

"Would you like to dance?" I made sure to articulate every word the same way Mara had said them when she was teaching Luca what he should say to a girl.

He blinked.

He blinked again.

One more time.

I made sure that I was holding his gaze, daring him to look away. My eyes willed him to say yes.

I wanted him to say yes.

I *needed* him to say yes.

But I was asking a boy to dance with me. Also a boy.

I didn't have much of a chance.

There was too much silence, and my palms had started to sweat. I needed a yes or a no.

Bloody hell, please say yes, Luca. Please.

Luca tore his eyes away from me and stood up.

My heart dislodged itself from where it sat between my lungs, and plummeted down into my stomach where acid was eating away at it.

I was done for.

That was a mistake. I shouldn't have-

He held out a hand.

I couldn't take it. I was glued to the ground, afraid that if I got up, it'd make me face the reality of what I asked.

I asked a boy to dance with me.

What the bloody hell was I-

"You are going to sit there, or dance with me?"

That was all I needed. My heart flew out from my stomach, putting itself right back where it was supposed to be. I almost gripped his hand to quickly as I got up.

"You know how to dance?" I asked him.

He nodded.

"Alright then, uh," I started to outstretch my hand to his, but then pulled back, second guessing myself. I extended the shaky hand again.

Should I grab his waist? Should I put my hand on his shoulder?

Bloody hell why was this so difficult?

But then, Luca hesitantly reached for one of my hands, positioning my other one on his shoulder, and then he snaked his arm around my waist, and just when I thought he was finished, he tightened his grip on me, pulling me flush up against him.

He was taller than me.

But not by much, and I found myself getting lost in the green and brown flecked eyes that were gazing intently at me.

"What do we do now?" he breathed out.

It made me smile a little at how nervous he was, his grip on my waist shaky, "I believe this is the part where we start to dance."

I must have spoken too quickly, because Luca had a look of confusion on his face again. I didn't try to clarify, I just started to sway back and forth, hoping he'd catch on.

He did, and then we were dancing.

There was no music except for the crickets chirping away without a care in the world. No light other than the moon, which cast a white glow across our face. From that second forward, everything was a blur.

Every spin we did, every time he twirled me, all the times he made me laugh, his smile as we tried to figure out how to dance together, trying to find a rhythm, his eyes that looked nervous after he'd stepped on my toe. Those were the only things that I'd remembered.

The hay bale vanished into nothingness. The grass was gone. The field was non-existent. Everything was a mess of color, merging together as if I was surrounded by paint that had been blended together. There was no shape to our surroundings. Just blobs and blurs.

And that was okay.

Because there were other things that were more important, that refused to blur. The image of him smiling at me in that nervous, I feel like I'm going to screw up, way. The way his breath fanned the tips of my hair, making the hair on my back rise.

My favorite though, was the way when I gave him that look that could make him shiver, he'd look down at the ground, or couldn't think straight enough to understand what his feet were doing, and forget which way we were swaying. How his cheeks heated up after I looked at him in a way I hadn't looked at anyone else.

I should have stopped what we were doing. I should have said it was weird. I should have said we shouldn't have been dancing. That two boys shouldn't be dancing in the middle of a field at night together.

But I couldn't bring myself to, because though what we were doing might have been wrong, it felt so right.

And I didn't know what that meant.

October 7th, 1943, 12:15am, Falmouth,
Cornwall, England.
Mara

I was smiling.

I was *fottutamente* smiling.

The kiss with Will kept replaying in my head.

It hadn't done that when I kissed Marco for the first time.

I was lying on my bed, gaze trained up at the ceiling, smiling like someone in the asylum.

My door swung open, and when I recognized Luca standing in the door frame, I couldn't stop myself from talking.

"I kissed Will," I blurted, snapping up to a sitting position.

"You kissed the English boy?" He raised an eyebrow.

"Yes."

Luca scoffed, "If *Nonna* has told you once, she's told you a thousand times-"

I couldn't help but roll my eyes, "Don't ruin the blood, *si, si, io so*. But *Nonna's* a Fascist."

He shrugged, "Yeah, well she always did what others told her to do."

"Probably why she hated me."

Luca laughed, "She didn't hate you."

"Really? That woman wanted to murder me half the time, and break my bones and mold me into a different person the other half. I consider that a hatred of my personality."

Nonna wasn't my relative, but she was Luca's, and therefore by default, that made her family. And just like *famiglia,* she always needed to have some opinion on my life. Especially me being too headstrong. I'd go to work in the fields with Luca, and she'd make sure to say, 'Ah, *bambina,* you should be finding yourself a husband, not busying yourself with a man's work.' To which I'd always respond, 'Well *Nonna,* if these crops don't get harvested there will be no food for my husband to eat.'

And then of course the times she'd talk about marriage. 'Aye, Mara, you must marry a good Italian boy. Do not let foreigners seduce you into their traps and have their babies. You don't want a blonde baby do you?'

Me being the smartass that I was would reply, '*Nonna,* I have no control over how a baby turns out.'

She'd give me that look, the look that said she wanted to chase me out of the house with a broom, and say, '*Cosa intendi,* you don't have control over how it turns out? If you marry an Italian boy, then you will have brown haired brown eyed babies, and they will have proud *Italiano* features.'

I'd then proceed to dig my own grave with the line, 'Well, *Nonna,* what if I just skip marriage and go straight to the baby making?'

Her face would twist and knot into an ugly snarl, and that was when I'd make my escape, waving goodbye before darting out the door and into the safety of the fields. *Nonna* never left the house anyway, she wouldn't have been able to hurt me outside.

Though I could still hear her curses playing in my ear, telling me I was going to burn in hell for my stubbornness.

Luca came to sit on the bed next to me, breaking me out of the memories, "Just be careful okay? English boys are odd."

"Well, they could say the same about Italians," I smirked.

There was a silence for a second before Luca nudged me, "So tell me about this Will."

My mind circled back to the kiss, and I couldn't help but sigh, falling onto the bed. Luca followed suit next to me.

"That amazing, huh?"

"Shut up."

"How far did you get?"

I looked over at him, "What are you talking about?"

"When you kissed, did you..."

Oh.

Ohhhh.

"*Dio*, no, we just talked, then we kissed, then we kissed again, and then that's when we decided to head back because it was getting late."

Luca smirked, "Whatever you say."

We laid in silence for a second.

"You two would make great little half Italian babies," he said with a smirk.

I gasped, "Luca!" I punched him in the arm.

"I'm just saying, the blue eyes paired with your skin and hair. They'd be movie stars."

I couldn't help laugh before shaking my head, "Well, you know what I always said to *Nonna,* I could always just skip marriage."

Now it was Luca's turn to gasp, "*Mara Donata Maria Seraphina Amalia Bianco,* what would your parents say?"

I shrugged, "I have no idea, they're dead, I'm well past asking for permission."

He laughed to himself, "I guess so."

I looked up at the ceiling, imagining two little kids running around a large house with dark brown hair, olive skin, and light blue eyes.

"Will and I would have really cute babies, wouldn't we?"

"Yes, yes you would."

There was a pause for a second.

"Thanks for this," I said, my voice only a whisper.

"For what? Getting you to picture yourself having babies with a guy you met two days ago?"

"No, for talking about this stuff with me. No one else does."

"Well, you've never tried talking to anyone else."

"We lived in a small town in Southern Italy. Not only did word spread around fast, but no one had anything else to do but talk. Remember what happened when I told a girl about Marco and I?"

Luca sucked in a breath, "Yeah, that wasn't good."

"Yeah, you're telling me, a day later I had a *nonna* coming up to me yelling to save myself until marriage or face Satan in Hell."

"About ready to throw a bible at your face if I remember right."

"Yup."

"Old ladies and their Catholicism," he said, laughter lacing his voice.

I scoffed, "Says the guy who's still clinging onto the bible for dear life."

He smiled, "Yeah, I guess you're right."

Another pause.

"What would it be like to die and go to Hell? I imagine half the population of Earth is going to end up there," I asked.

"You'd be stuck with Mussolini and Hitler when they die, and probably Marco."

"Yeah, that'd be *merda*."

"But, you'd be surrounded by fire and lava, and Satan."

I pursed my lips, "Always wanted to have a talk with that guy."

Luca smirked, "So, in conclusion-"

"There are advantages and disadvantages to Hell."

Luca laughed before getting up from the bed. He grabbed my legs that were dangling off, and spun me around gently so my whole body was lying on the bed. He lifted my torso, and then my legs, moving the blanket out from under me, only to drape it over my body moments later.

"*Buona notte, Mara.*"

"*Buona notte, Luca,*" I muttered as the warmth of the blanket surrounded me, and as soon as I started to huddle under it, I let out a hiss. My gun was at an odd angle under my pillow, making my neck hurt. I groaned and shifted it a little and I felt my neck relax. Black seized my vision and my eyes slowly started to close, giving into sleep.

I couldn't help being afraid of what nightmares might plague my night.

CHAPTER 12

October 7th, 1943, 9:43am, Falmouth, Cornwall, England
Mara

It was raining hard. The runoff had muddied the road leading to the center of town, so on Sunday, we were all stuck in the house because we couldn't get to church. Because that's what people did on Sunday, they went to church and prayed away their sins. Though as soon as they left the church, they would continue to sin, because that was all people could do these days. But they'd still pray because in the end, that was what they thought would save their soul from damnation.

Even now, the Smithsons were in the living room, Luca with them, praying.

I couldn't do it.

I couldn't sit there and listen to them whisper about some immortal person that lived in the clouds. Part of me knew it was useless. I knew no matter how much I put my hands together and conversed with nothingness, it wouldn't be enough. There was a point of no return for sin, and I had passed that mark a long time ago.

So I stayed in my room that morning, pretending I was sleeping to avoid the miserable action of praying.

The railroad station had been madness the few days after the dance. I'd been working on everything from loading coal onto trains, to covering the place in new paint. I was exhausted. The time change was becoming less noticeable, however. Even though we were only a few hours behind *Italia,* it was still enough to leave me miserably tired by the end of the day.

I sat at my window, looking out into the distance. The sea was angry, knotting in various twists and turns as rain pelted down onto it.

My foot was tapping against the side of the bench, and as I looked around the room that had been quite large a moment ago, it seemed like it was getting smaller and smaller.

I hated being cooped up inside all day. When I was working, I was outside. I wasn't cooped up. I was closer to freedom outdoors. But now, it was Sunday, and the station didn't operate on Sundays.

The walls were closing in.

My hands were shaking, needing to be doing something other than nothing, drawn to the cool metal under my pillow. I needed to clear my head.

I needed to think, and breathe, and get out of the house, because if I stayed any longer not doing anything, I was certain I would have another attack. And having a distressed Italian in your house wasn't what you wanted. Especially when that Italian has access to a gun, while having a panic attack.

Those two didn't exactly go together well.

My hands gripped the gun in my hand, pulling it out from under the pillow. I put it in the waistband of my straight khaki pants and fumbled with my boots before sliding on my jacket.

I needed to get out of the house.

Rain helped to calm people down, or so I'd heard. It

could do the same for me, right? At least, rain plus shooting things seemed calming to me.

I opened my window, the sound of water hitting the roof plinking in my ear as I climbed down the house. The walls were slippery this time, and I had to keep a tight grip on the window sill and then the ivy so I wouldn't fall.

I made my way to the open field. The expanse of green turned murky as I jumped the wooden and stone fence, fog drifting through the air. I couldn't help but smile. No walls. No small spaces. Just freedom.

I looked at a hay bale down range, the thin fog doing little to hide it, and took my gun out, holding it in front of me with both hands. My eyes closed as my finger started to tighten on the trigger. But something was stopping me from taking the shot and my finger was frozen in its place. My hands started to shake. I tried to pull the trigger again, but I couldn't move.

I couldn't do it.

I couldn't shoot the damn gun.

I put my hand down, letting out a breath through my nose. What was going on?

Was I having an attack?

I checked my breathing, which though shaky, was not ragged and uncontrollable. Was not being able to shoot a gun a form of shell-shock? I didn't think so. If anything, shell-shock just made me more dependent on the gun.

So why couldn't I pull the trigger?

I didn't have adrenaline pumping through my veins like I usually did when I shot.

Maybe I didn't have it in me.

No.

That couldn't be it.

I'd killed people with that gun.

A hay bale was nothing compared to that.

I was going to pull the trigger.

I *needed* to pull the trigger.

I raised the gun again, one handed this time, and turned away before looking back at my target.

Nice and steady.

A long breath escaped my lips, my hand steadier than before. The rain sounded like a distant whisper as everything around me disappeared. Just me, and the hay bale, and the grass that was high enough to tickle my legs.

My hand tightened on the trigger.

Three, two, o-

"Mara?"

I whipped around, muscle memory taking over as I turned the gun to face whomever was talking.

There was a black haired boy standing underneath an umbrella, face covered in shadow. His arms shot up defensively, "Woah, Mara, it's me, Will."

Will.

Oh *fanculo*.

My finger loosened on the trigger, and I quickly lowered the gun, tucking it into my waistband. I wiped the rain from my face and blinked.

He saw the gun.

"Oh, Will, hey, uh, what are you doing out here?"

He smiled, "Well, I was goin' to clear my 'ead, but it's kind of 'ard to do that when someone points a gun to my chest."

I looked down, "Oh."

"If you don't mind me askin'-"

I blinked, "I do." The words came out pointed and cold, which wasn't intended, but it was how I felt. I didn't want to explain anything. I didn't want to tell Will I had a gun because I'd killed people with it.

I hadn't told him that part of being in the Resistance. I hoped it was implied, but I doubted it was.

He pursed his lips and nodded, "Okay, that's alright. What are you doin' out 'ere on this *sunny* day anyhow?"

I couldn't help smiling at that, "Clearing my head."

"While it's rainin'?"

"You were doing the same thing."

"Yes, but I 'ave an umbrella, there's a difference between yours and mine," he said, eyes going to where the gun was tucked away.

"Yeah, I guess so."

He blinked. He was wearing almost the exact same thing he always wore, and his hair was a little damp, but not completely drenched like how mine was. His icy blue eyes looked brighter with the dark cloud covered sky hanging over us.

He motioned towards himself with the umbrella as if I should go over to him, but I stayed where I was. I didn't know if I should or not.

He smiled, "Well, what are you waitin' for? Do you want to keep gettin' buckets of water dumped on you?"

"Is that an invitation?"

Will let out a breath and walked over to me, holding the large black umbrella over my head, "Yes, yes it is," he said with a smile.

In that moment I noticed just how close he really was to me. His breath fanned my neck, and I couldn't help shifting my face so that I could see him out of the corner of my eye.

"Hi," I whispered.

"'Ello there."

Will's eyes flickered to my lips before he leaned down

and pressed a soft kiss to them, while his arm wrapped around my shoulders, pulling me closer to him, "I missed you, Mara."

"Missed you too."

"Sorry I couldn't see you for the past few days, I 'ad to work at my grandpa's, we've been swamped with people comin' in with colds and such."

That made my mind relax a bit.

After the party, and the kiss, I hadn't seen Will, and I'd started to get nervous, Luca's words about English boys working their way into my mind.

"You're not going to get me sick are you?" I asked, stepping back a little.

He laughed, "If I was, d'you think I'd be 'ere? I mean, I'd probably still be 'ere, but that's besides the point. Point is I'm not sick."

I just smiled at Will's rambling before he motioned towards the fence, "'Ow's about we sit down?"

"That sounds lovely."

As we sat down on the wooden fence, I noticed something silver hanging out of his coat pocket, a cross attached to a string of beads.

A rosary.

I felt myself tense at the thing I was all too familiar with.

I pointed at it, "You believe in God?"

Will looked at me confused for a second at the blunt comment, and then noticed my eyes trained on the rosary in his pocket, "Oh," he exclaimed, pulling it out to show me, "Yeah, I suppose I do. You?"

I paused, my eyes gazing out into the dissipating fog, "No. When you've seen innocent people get killed because a soldier felt like it, you find it hard to believe that there's someone watching out for you."

His hand moved from the wood fence, to on top of mine, and he gripped it tight.

"But you've gotta stop and wonder sometimes that there must be somethin' out there watchin' out for you."

I shrugged, locking eyes with him, "Any God I could learn to believe in should be watching out for everyone. God shouldn't be sitting by watching this world rip itself apart because of hate and violence. No, my God would have stopped this."

Will blinked, before scooting closer to me, placing both our hands on his leg.

"You can believe whatever you want, Mara, but in this war, everyone needs to have faith in somethin'."

My hands started shaking a little, and I was glad for his hand holding at least one of them to cover up the tremors. My other hand though wouldn't stop its fidgeting.

I needed to shoot.

My hand went to the gun in my waistband and I pulled it out. Will looked at it skeptically, but relaxed a little when I pointed it off into the distance, aiming for the first hay bale in front of me, about thirty meters away.

I closed one eye, put my finger on the trigger, and glanced back at those icy blue eyes.

"Oh, I have faith. Faith in my ability to keep myself alive."

My finger tightened on the trigger, and a loud bang echoed across the open field.

I looked at my shot, and I watched the hay bale cave in the middle because of the hole I blasted through.

My jaw clenched, "And that's how I keep myself alive."

Will's eyes widened, "Well, it seems my girl's an expert shot."

I laughed a little before deciding I should circle back to the faith thing.

Wait, did he call me his girl?

I set my gun in my lap, one hand on the grip, and the other holding his, "I understand your faith, Will, I just haven't seen anything that would prove God is a good being."

"You never know when 'e'll reveal 'imself to you, Mara, you just gotta wait."

I smirked, "Yeah, I'm not exactly the waiting type."

Will chuckled before taking his arm and wrapping it around my shoulders, my hand still in his, "That so?"

"Yup."

We sat there for a second under the umbrella, listening to the sound of rain hitting the top. Parts of the green field were starting to get lit up with small spots of sun shining through the rain clouds.

I opened my mouth, breaking the peaceful silence, "So when did you decide that I was your girl?"

He blinked, "Uh... Well, I'd 'oped the kiss would 'ave done that for you, but okay, I can formally ask."

"Is that what happens here? You just ask?"

"Well 'ow does it 'appen in Italy?"

"Oh, well, you have to get approval from the town, and then the girl's grandmother, very important, and then the father-"

"Okay, so I'll go to Italy when this is all over and ask your town, your grandmother, and your father for their approval."

I laughed a little at his determination and his playful demeanor.

"Well, I mean, you can skip my parents, they're dead, died in an ENR raid," I said with a sad smile, before my face fell thinking about the rest of the people I left behind, "Who knows about the others."

He blinked, looking shocked, "Wait, your parents are dead?"

I nodded, "Yup. It's fine though, I'm okay."

"'Ow are you okay?"

"It happened a while ago, I've learned to move on."

That felt easier to say than the truth. Because it hadn't happened a while ago, it was only about five months before, around the time that I left to join the Resistance. I'd moved on, but only because I wasn't special. There were a lot of other kids who went through the same thing as I did, and much younger ages. It was a reality of the war. People dying wasn't new anymore. People living, well, that was a myth.

"I'm sorry Mar-"

"Mara!"

My head whipped around, almost falling off the fence as I did. James was standing there in the pouring rain, drenched and barefoot, a couple yards away, and the way his chest heaved up and down, told me something was wrong.

"James, what happened?"

"It's Luca. He- I don't know, there was a loud noise, and he started breathing heavy. I don't know. I think he's having some sort of-"

I gripped my gun in my hand, taking it from my lap before leaping off the fence. Tucking the gun back into my waistband, under my shirt, I assured myself James hadn't seen it when my back was to him.

I started heading towards the blonde. "Attack. He's having an attack," I looked back at Will, "I have to go, I'm sorry. Luca needs me."

He nodded, "No, yeah, you go. I'll find a way to see you again," he said, giving me a smile before I took off sprinting in the rain, racing passed James.

"Hurry," I called back to him, as I ran back towards the house.

Merda, Luca heard the shot. That was the trigger. This was my fault.

This was what I didn't want, I didn't want one of us to panic with the Smithsons there. Because being an Italian was one thing, being a crazy Italian was another.

James

I'd been teaching Luca how to play spades after Aunt Hester and Uncle George had finished praying with us and they'd left the parlor. Uncle George was taking a nap, and Aunt Hester was reciting the Bible in her small study.

And all of a sudden, right as I was about to throw down an ace of clubs, a loud noise rang out through the parlor.

BANG!

That's when it happened. Luca tensed, his hands started to quiver and shake, and his cards slipped from his grasp.

I'd asked him if he was alright, but he didn't reply, he just sat on the couch, shaking, his eyes trained on something in front of him.

I didn't know what to do, I'd never seen someone do this before. I'd run to get Mara, but she wasn't in her room. I went outside, seeing if she was around, and I found her sitting on the fence with Will.

Now, I was drenched with water, shivering in the parlor, as Mara dropped down in front of Luca as he continued to shake.

Her hands, damp from the rain flew to his, and she just started uttering phrases in Italian.

"*Tu bene, sei al sicuro. Siamo in Inghilterra, sei al sicuro. Nessuno può farti del male. Respiro. Respiro. Shhhh. Sono qui. Shhhh.*"

I watched as Luca's whole body kept shivering, and his breathing started to become audible. I felt helpless standing there. I wanted to do something. I needed to do something.

So I came and sat next to him on the sofa, in front of Mara, who didn't give me a second glance.

She kept talking to Luca, "*Anche* James *e qui. Shhhhh.*"

One of her hands left his own and came up to hold his shoulder. The hand she wasn't holding started to shake and I watched as Luca muttered something to her, something I couldn't understand. Mara nodded almost to herself before gazing up at me with the same hazel eyes Luca had.

"Can you?"

"Can I what?"

"I need to be able to hold both his hands so he doesn't do anything stupid," She said, her voice a whisper, but sharp. I saw a look of fear in her eyes, but the way she was handling it, it didn't seem like it was the first time this had happened.

I still wasn't catching on, and Mara huffed, aggravated, quickly gripping my hand and pulled. It made me stumble from my spot beside Luca and got me to sit up. She pointed to a spot behind the couch and I moved to where I was behind Luca. Mara motioned for me to place my hands on his shoulders.

Oh.

I nodded to show that I understood, gently placing

both hands on him as Mara kept whispering. It went on for a few seconds before I felt once again helpless, considering Luca hadn't stopped shaking, his breath still coming out unsteady. Then I remembered something my mum used to do when I was little when I'd have a nightmare and I couldn't go back to sleep.

One of my hands drifted down from his shoulder, to the center of Luca's back and my fingers started to trace circles across the white fabric of his shirt.

Slowly, I felt his shoulders lose their tension, and his breathing started to slow.

"*Sto bene, sto bene,*" he said, looking up at us both, his eyes lingering on mine a little while longer, and I realized that my hands were still on his back and shoulder. I removed them, stuffing my hands into my pockets. I couldn't help but feel my face flush red, and I turned, starting to make my way to the kitchen. There was no specific reason, other than to get away from Luca's gaze.

Though, Mara grabbed my arm and stared at me with one of the most serious faces I'd seen.

Stone cold.

"You don't tell anyone about this, you understand?"

I hesitated, but I noticed when I did, her grip tightened around my arm, so I nodded, "Yes, I won't tell anyone."

"Thank you."

She stood up, pulling me away from Luca.

"He's going to have to lie down for a little while to make sure he doesn't start panicking again. It happens sometimes. But uh, I need you to watch him," she whispered.

"Why can't you?"

She shrugged, "He doesn't like it when I do. Hates the fact that I actually give a *merda.*" She articulated the last part, raising her voice so he could hear her. It made Luca huff a little before she continued, "So maybe he'll tolerate you watching him."

I nodded, "Yeah, uh, of course."

"I'll be in my room in case he starts having an attack again. Just watch his breathing and his hands for shaking."

"Got it."

"*Grazie mille*," Mara said, slipping into Italian, which seemed like what she did when she was tired, exhausted, or when something like that happened.

A day ago when she was so beat from working at the station, she just started speaking Italian, not even bothering to translate. According to her, the translating had gotten easier. She knew the words, it was just how fast she could put them all together.

I moved towards Luca and held out a hand for him to take, which he did, and I pulled him up from the couch. It was almost as if he was in a daze as we made our way up the stairs and into my room. It wasn't long after I laid him down on his bed that I saw his eyes flutter shut, giving into sleep.

Luca

Everything was dark.

Dark, and terrifying.

I was hearing people scream.

Crying.

Loud gunshots around me.

Something warm on my hands, on my body, everywhere.

Blood?

I couldn't see anything. I could just hear, and feel, and

smell the burning, acrid air.

A baby crying in the distance.

The sound of sirens.

Words in a harsh language that sounded familiar.

Words that made me want to run as fast as I could.

And-

"Luca?"

A voice with a British accent?

Che cosa?

"Luca, wake up."

My eyes snapped open, and I instinctively bolted up in bed. Startled.

A hand came onto my chest to keep me from flying out of the room, I probably looked like I wanted to. My eyes followed the hand, to the arm, to the body, and that body was James.

I looked at the hand, and then his eyes, and then back down at the hand, which was right where my shirt had been unbuttoned.

"James," I whispered, almost as a warning.

He looked at his hand on my skin, and quickly pulled away before he pointed at me. James twisted back and forth over and over again with his eyes closed, and then let out a few grunts and cries.

Oh.

I was talking in my sleep.

Wait, why was I asleep?

"What...happened?" I said, struggling to put a sentence together.

James blinked, "You don't...?"

I shook my head.

My mind was blank. The last thing I remembered was dinner the night before. I had no idea how I wound up in bed, with James sitting in a chair next to me.

He let out a sigh, his deep eyes filled with something that I hadn't seen from him since we got here.

Concern maybe?

"You uh, had an attack."

"*Che cosa?*"

James blinked for a second, huffing, and then pointed at me before crouching into a ball still sitting on the chair, and rocking back and forth.

Oh *merda.*

"*Attacco.*"

He went back to how he was sitting before, and looked at me, nodding, "Yeah. An attacco."

It made me want to laugh at how poor his pronunciation was this time, but the way James looked at me made me stop myself.

He looked serious.

He looked concerned.

He looked scared.

His eyes swirling with questions it seemed, but he was only able to get out one.

"Does it happen often?"

My brain racked with translating, racing to put words together.

How the *diavolo* did Mara manage to do this so fast?

And finally, everything clicked.

"Sometimes. In *Italia,* with the war. Guns. *Boom,*" I couldn't find any other way to put it. At least not in English, "Mara does too."

"She does?"

I nodded after a second, taking me a bit to understand, "What we have seen, is a lot. We hear thing, like gunshot, and panic." I looked at the ground for a second, "Take us back to war."

My hands were shaking. I knew that. I looked down at them, trying to will them to stop. It usually happened after one of my attacks, the shock of everything and the adrenaline pumping through my veins a main cause of the tremors.

Two hands came around my shaking ones and I looked up at Jame's eyes that appeared to have two small oceans in them.

"I'm sorry," I whispered. I was acting pathetic. I had attacks all the time. I didn't need someone coaching me through the aftermath of it.

I tried shrugging off his hands, trying to get up, but James grabbed my arm, sitting me back down on the bed.

"You have nothing to be sorry for, Luca."

The way he said my name sent a shiver up my spine.

I loved the way he said it.

The accent, how his eyes bore into mine.

"You do not have to hold hand, I am fine."

"I want to."

"You do not have to."

"I want to," he repeated, scooting the chair he was sitting in closer to my bed.

We were within a few centimeters from each other, to the point where it was hard to focus on both of his eyes. I had to shift between the two before deciding to look down at our hands.

"I'm here for you, Luca. I know we don't know each other very well, but you can trust me. Alright? I'm right here whenever you need me."

Pause.

Put the words together like puzzle pieces.

Try again.

Over and over, running different possibilities in my mind, and then it hit me.

He was there for me. He was there for me when I needed him.

Something in my stomach started to heat up, and from the inside, something was tickling me.

Farfalle.

Aspetta... Farfalle?

Wait... Butterflies?

That wasn't possible. I didn't get butterflies. I didn't get butterflies for a English boy who looked like a *Nazista*. I didn't get butterflies for a *boy*.

But here I was, feeling the fluttering in my stomach and all I could think about was how he said he was right there whenever I needed him.

"I need you now, uh, here."

James's eyes shone bright, and he nodded, "Of course. I'm here."

What I wanted to say was simply: I need you.

But I didn't know if I was ready to say something like that. I didn't even know what saying something like that meant.

More importantly, I wasn't sure I was ready to understand why the butterflies in my stomach were there.

Especially if they made me want to say that.

I need you.

I didn't know what it was about him that made my stomach do flips.

Maybe it was his eyes. Or the way he smiled at me. Or the way we'd danced with each other a few nights ago. Maybe it so happened to be the way that when his hands were holding mine, when we were this close, I felt safe.

Which was a feeling I hadn't felt in a very long time.

CHAPTER 13

October 11th, 1943, 3:21pm, Falmouth, Cornwall, England
Luca

My arms were screaming at me as I drove the shovel into the basin of coal once again and sweat was starting to drip down my back. Why was it this hot out?

Why the hell wasn't Mara doing this? Something about replacing some rotting wood on part of the ticket booth, and then she had to go help get some more bags of coal from a shipment coming into the station. So James and I were stuck shoveling the black rocks into every train that came through.

It was just supposed to be me, but he had offered to help, Mara had said it was because no sane man would attempt to do the work on their own.

Though, she could do it herself.

But Mara wasn't exactly the sanest person I'd ever met.

I wasn't going to deny how it was taking half the time to fill each train up with coal with James's help. It was silent between us, other than the constant digging into the coal that our two shovels were doing. I'd tried to string together sentences early on, but then gave up trying to translate.

I drove my shovel into the coal when the fuel car looked like it was filled and gave a thumbs up to the conductor of the train, something James had done for the first one that went through here.

The train gave a blast, and started moving on to Plymouth station. We were just a coal stop for them. No one got off, and no one got on.

James did the same as me, putting his shovel into the mound of black rock, and smiled through labored breaths.

I didn't say anything.

I felt like I should.

It was as if words were on the tip of my tongue but I couldn't get them out. Like my mouth was stitched shut. It felt weird, wanting to say something, and having no idea what to say, or how to say it.

"Where's a cricket when you need one, right?" James said, his voice light.

My mind raked for answers, some of the words seemed familiar. Some of them didn't. Together, it was just a long string of nothing.

I shook my head, realizing I'd been just staring at him for the last few seconds and not really saying anything.

"*Non capisco, mi dispiace.*"

James laughed before shaking his head, waving his hand as if to say it didn't matter.

There was a silence once again as the clouds covered the sun, stopping the rays from getting to my skin. It made my body relax a little. That was, until I remembered the growing quiet between James and I.

What could I really say?

Well, a lot of things if I actually spoke his language, or he spoke more of mine.

But instead of opening my mouth again and trying to get a word out, I just gave him a thumbs up, which was met with his smile and another thumbs up. I tried not to look at his eyes, keeping my own trained on his shoulder, or his nose, but never his eyes. If I looked at his eyes, it'd remind me of the feeling I got when I saw him.

And that feeling, well, it wasn't normal.

So I just focused on wiping the sweat from my face, stopping the beads from dripping down, my eyes anywhere but his.

I knew he was watching me. I felt the two ocean eyes drilling into the side of my face.

"Uh, Luca, you've got something, uh-"

I raised my eyebrows as if asking what was wrong and he shook his head again before getting closer to me.

He held out a hand that told me to stay where I was, even though every step closer he took was one more step I wanted to take back. I shoved my hands into my pockets as he brought a soot covered hand closer to my face. A pause for a second, and I saw something flash in his eyes, something that made me weary. It was the same kind of glint Mara got when she was going to push me into a pile of hay when we were younger.

Then I felt a warm hand run down my face, smearing the coal dust from his hand onto my forehead, nose, and cheeks.

James jumped back a little, chuckling at my wide eyed, jaw dropped reaction.

"Stop," I was able to get out, but couldn't help a small smile start to play at my lips.

"I did," he said, trying to control his laughter at my ash covered face.

I attempted to wipe the stuff off but I was just making it worse seeing as my own palms were turning black with the remnants of coal.

I let out a frustrated huff as James's laughter became louder in my ears, and my eyes locked with his for a second. He was trying to regain his breath, but it wasn't working.

Lightbulb.

My smile grew into a smirk, which made his own eyes turn from amused, to cautious.

"Luca? What are you gonna-"

Too late.

I gripped his hand, pulling him towards me, only to streak my hand down the side of his face, even getting some of his blonde *Nazista* hair dirty, turning it ashy.

The side of his face had long black stripes on it from my fingers and I laughed.

"It's not funny."

I nodded, "This is funny."

James shook his head, "You're gonna get it, Luca."

"Non capis-"

And then I felt something hard hit my chest, sending me stumbling back into the basin of coal. I closed my eyes, grunting with how the coal shifted around me, digging into places on my back. I felt like I was going to sink.

But I didn't.

Instead, I felt a hand on my face again, running up and down, and a little bit of coal got in my mouth.

My eyes snapped open to see James on top of me, a boy-ish smile plastered to his lips.

I tried to push him off as he was intent on turning my white shirt black. I couldn't help smiling while rubbing my hand in the coal to the side of me. I flung my arm up to hit James on his arm, leaving a dark handprint on his creme colored shirt.

A flurry of flailing arms, trying to hit each other, and

leave the other a sooty mess, were what followed, mixed with obnoxious laughter.

And then, his eyes caught mine, and all of that stopped. I froze. My breath caught in my throat. I wasn't breathing. I was drowning in his eyes.

"What the bloody hell are you boys doing?"

James turned away, scrambling off me. But when he stood, his eyes kept shifting between me on the ground, and his uncle a few yards away.

Mr. Smithson had a smile on his face, as if he was laughing at the whole situation, but he only saw two boys throwing coal around.

I saw something much worse.

The realization hit me just as if a piece of coal had been flung at my head.

James had been on top of me, his hands were all over my body, and my hands were all over his.

The thought both scared me and sent a flutter through my stomach.

It overwhelmed me. So much so that I couldn't get up off the ground. I would probably fall if I did. So I just sat there as Mara came to see what was going on.

She had a smirk on her face as she looked in between James and I.

"You look like a chimney sweep," she said to me in Italian, making me chuckle to myself, almost forgetting my thoughts.

I had ash all over my white shirt and the brown pants I was wearing, ruining the color. No doubt it was in my hair and all over my face.

I turned to James to see what kind of damage I had caused. His hair was covered in the coal dust, turning some parts of it black, while his clothes were in the same state as mine.

"Alright you two, you've had your fun, get yourselves cleaned up before we go home so Hester doesn't kill the both of you."

James nodded, but I turned to Mara for help, which she gave by translating.

We both watched as Mr. Smithson left, while Mara lingered for a moment with a look on her face. It was like she was trying to solve a puzzle. The look told me the gears were turning in her mind. I just couldn't tell what she was trying to figure out, and that scared me.

James turned back to me once Mara had left, and our eyes locked. The thoughts I was having before Mara started talking rushed back as I got lost in the blue. I couldn't breathe. But he seemed fine.

I watched as a hand outstretched, James's attempt at helping me up. I stared at it for a second, not moving.

"Are you going to sit there all day?"

Pause.

Translate.

Think through.

I understood.

But I did want to sit there all day, because standing up meant I had to take his hand.

I'd have to touch him again.

And I didn't know if my body would let me let go of his hand if I took it.

Che cazzo sta succedendo?

What the fuck was going on?

The worst part was I knew exactly what was going on.

And that terrified me.

But I needed to get cleaned up and I needed help getting up.

I quickly grasped James's hand, and he pulled. I shot up, almost colliding with his chest.

I stood there for a second, trying to memorize how his hand felt in mine. How the softness of his palm wasn't there now, instead it was roughed up from holding the shovel. His hand was warm, and it felt like mine fit perfectly in his, like two puzzle pieces.

I realized just how close we were, to the point where our faces were almost touching.

Too close.

Way too close.

I pulled back and dropped his hand quickly, scrambling out of the coal pit. When I set my feet on the ground, I closed my eyes for a second, trying to calm my racing thoughts.

"You alright?" James asked, making my eyes snap open.

I looked at him, nodding. No matter how untrue it was. No matter how much I really wanted to say, no, I just nodded.

He smiled. It was the smile that knocked the breath out of me, one that made me forget where I was. So much so that I didn't realize he was walking away from me until he paused and looked back at me.

"Luca, you coming?" He motioned for me to follow him.

I nodded, snapping out of whatever trance I was in and trapsed after James. We went around the station, towards the side that backed up to a large outcrop of trees, and there was a water spout that shot out of the building, a hose attached to it.

I stood back a little, watching as James turned on the water, the cold stream pouring onto the dirt, turning it to mud. He paused for a second, taking a deep breath before he put his head under the running water. He took a hand and rinsed off his face and hair.

I tried not to look, but I was fixated with him. I couldn't look away.

And when he pulled away from the water, his hair wet, no more pomade in it, pieces getting in his eyes, and sticking to his forehead, my heart sped up.

Faster and faster.

I knew why, and it scared me.

These feelings I had, they weren't supposed to be there.

They weren't supposed to be for him.

They weren't supposed to be for a *him*.

These things I was thinking. The things I felt when he looked at me. They were bad, they weren't right.

But if they weren't right, then why were they so strong that every centimeter of my body wanted to feel them all the time, every second of the day and night?

James

I watched him looking at me.

I knew he was watching me. I knew he wasn't breathing right. I knew he was panicking. I had seen the look in his eyes. But I didn't know why there was cause for panic.

I was cold.

The water was freezing, and it was running down my back.

I outstretched my arm, the hose in my hand, my hands still covered in black, but it was a shadow of what it had been before.

"Come on, your turn."

Luca slowly reached his hand to grip it, and took a breath before tipping it over his head. He bent forward, and I watched as the muscles under his shirt tensed with the chill of the water.

It took about three seconds for him to move away from the water, spluttering for air.

His shirt was soaked through, and it clung to him, wrapping around his muscles.

And with his hair plastered to his neck and to the sides of his face, hazel eyes fixated on my own blue ones, it made me hold my breath.

There was this feeling in my chest, like a warmth I got when I saw him, and although I didn't know what that meant, there was no denying I was drawn to him.

The way his eyes held my attention, the way he always unbuttoned the top buttons on his shirt, the way he'd furrow his eyebrows when he didn't understand what I was saying. How thick his accent was when he'd try to speak in English, and the melodic way he'd speak in Italian.

Maybe I was just fascinated by the fact he was Italian. I'd never known someone who wasn't English.

Or maybe it was something much more than that.

But I couldn't exactly place what I was feeling.

Perhaps because I'd never felt it before. This burning warmth in my chest, and the flip flops my stomach did when his hand was in mine.

But whatever it was, I really didn't want it to stop.

CHAPTER 14

**October 15th, 1943, 10:12am, Falmouth,
Cornwall, England**
Mara

Why did it have to rain?

Why did I have nothing to do? Again?

Mr. and Mrs. Smithson had to go out and wouldn't be back until late, so James, Luca, and I were supposed to have fun. But so far, there was no fun to be had.

I was currently battling Luca for the last few hundred lira we'd stashed, and the only way to get it, was to play poker.

My eyes shifted in between the two cards in the middle, my own, and Luca's *merdosa* poker face, which told me he was bluffing. All in for two hundred lira, and he was bluffing like *Nonna* trying to lie about how much she had to drink.

I kept a straight face as I turned over the last card.

An ace.

I had two aces already.

He was going to lose.

I went all in with my four hundred lira.

Luca gritted his teeth together. He knew I had a good hand. I only went all in when I knew I would win. Luca, on the other hand, never thought of what could happen if someone called his bluff.

I smirked, "You going to fold, Luca?"

"No."

"Huh, must be a great hand then."

"Yeah, it is."

Liar.

I nodded, "Alright, I'm calling."

He huffed and laid his cards out.

A five, a three, a ten, a nine, and a seven.

I threw down my own.

Two aces, a king, queen, and a ten.

"*Vafanculo*," Luca muttered under his breath as I took the crumpled lira into my hand and stuffed them into my pocket.

"Admit it, you're terrible at poker," I said smiling.

"Whatever, you're still the worst at Machiavelli."

I huffed, "Who said I sucked at that?"

"Everyone."

"And does everyone include the *cazzo* I just took two hundred lira from?"

"Rude," he said before grabbing a piece of paper he'd been doodling on. He'd always been good at drawing, it was what he did instead of paying attention when we were in school. He was best at drawing people. At first I'd been the person he'd drawn, but then he'd get mad at me because I couldn't sit still for over a minute. At one point he'd gotten nice graphite pencils from a cousin in *Roma* and would never go anywhere without one in his pocket and a small notebook.

All that had been given up when our town got hit by the raids. The soldiers tore through his house often, and once, he had been in the kitchen drawing and they took the art supplies. Any of his drawings were burned or torn to shreds.

He hadn't drawn since. At least, until now.

I wanted to ask him about it, but I stopped myself as I heard footsteps coming into the parlor, and looked up to see James crossing the threshold.

"What are you playing?" he asked.

"We *were* playing poker."

"Who won?"

I smiled, pulling out the money, "Me."

I glanced over at Luca, looking for any sign of wanting to kill me for taking the rest of his money. He didn't look pissed though. He wasn't even looking at me.

He was looking at James.

And James was looking back at him as if they didn't even remember I was there.

James smiled, one that would've made any girl around him swoon. I looked back at Luca, it seemed as if it made him swoon too. James's eyes flickered to the piece of paper and pen Luca had swiped, his eyes wide. His gaze snapped between me and the picture.

"Bloody hell, Luca. You draw?"

Luca blinked, unsure what to say. I huffed. Why couldn't he just magically wake up speaking fluent English one day?

"*Disegni?*" My attention then turned to James, "What the hell do you think he's doing right now?"

James let out a breath, "Right, yeah, of course. It's just, it's really good."

I looked back at Luca, "He likes the drawing."

Luca smiled a little, and showed me the sketch. It was of me, focused on the playing cards in my hand, my eyes furrowed in concentration.

I blinked, "You finally decided to start drawing me again?"

"Well, this was the only time you actually stayed still."

He did have a point.

James looked at him, "Maybe sometime you could draw me."

I translated. Luca went rigid as he shifted his gaze back to the blonde boy, mouth opened slightly as if he was going to say something, but couldn't. He just nodded.

Knock Knock Knockity Knock Knock.

The sound of the front door rang out through the parlor and I shot up out of the lounge chair I had been sitting in. I raced through the entryway and approached the door, hoping it was Mr. Smithson, needing some help around the house.

Fix something, move something, anything instead of sitting around.

But when I opened the door, it wasn't Mr. Smithson.

"I see this 'ouse 'as an angel residin' in it, huh?"

Cockney.

Will was standing with his arms crossed, hair and shirt damp from the rain. He leaned against the door frame with a smirk on his face and a look in his eyes that made me blush.

"What the hell are you doing here?"

"Lovely to see you too Mara. I'm 'ere, cause I 'eard the Smithsons were gonna be gone for the day."

"Where did you hear that?"

"Word travels fast around 'ere."

I found that hard to believe.

"Really?" I asked.

Will shook his head, "No, I just noticed someone else was runnin' the station when I stopped by. You bein' stuck in the Smithson's 'ouse was my best guess."

I laughed to myself, "Of course. Still, why are you

here?"

"Well- May I come in?" he asked as if that would add to the effect of why he was here.

I moved out of the doorway as an invitation, which he gladly took and stepped into the house. I waited for him to move past me, but as soon as he walked in, he spun and with some sort of masterful speed, I found myself pressed up against the wall.

Will was close, very close.

So close that the two ice blocks set in his eyes were the only things I could focus on.

That, and how close his lips were to mine.

"Will..." I said, trying to tell him without actually saying it, that it wasn't the time for this. Whatever *this* was. Especially seeing as my best friend and the boy who owned the house we were in were in the room to the side of us.

Will smirked, as if already aware of the people in the other room.

"Mara..." he drew out the word, sending a shiver down my spine, his breath fanning my lips.

I opened my mouth to say something. I wasn't quite sure what I would say, but I knew I wanted to say *something.* Though as soon as words tried to form on my tongue, a finger came up and pressed against the bottom of my chin, pushing my jaw closed.

Index finger still under my chin, Will's thumb touched my bottom lip, slowly moving back and forth, before he slowly ran the finger down, tugging on my mouth a little before letting his thumb fall. The finger still under my chin burned into my skin. It felt as if that single finger was bringing me closer and closer to him.

My eyes fluttered shut and my heart sped up, just like it

had the first time we kissed.

And finally, I felt Will's lips press against mine. Softly, as if they were barely even there.

As if I was being kissed by a ghost.

It was so different from the first time we kissed, but it still managed to stop time.

His arms wrapped around me, holding me close to him, and it felt like the room was spinning as he pulled away ever so slightly to whisper into my ear.

"I would kiss you 'arder, but I 'ave it on good authority the chaps in the other room wouldn't want to 'ear that."

I felt my face burn as his words hit my ears, and he smirked at my reaction, planting one last kiss on my cheek.

"Think we ought to say 'ello to the lads? Probably wonderin' where you went off to."

I nodded as if in a daze, my mind still on his lips softly pressing against mine.

Removing one of his arms from my waist, he guided me away from the wall, before dropping the lingering hand, letting me lead the way to the parlor.

I didn't know what I expected when I got back, but Luca and James as far apart as they could be on the couch wasn't it.

What the hell was going on with them?

Will elbowed my side, and I snapped out of trying to figure out what exactly was going on, instead clearing my throat to tell them that I was back.

Luca's eyes snapped up to me, and his shoulders that I didn't realize were so tense, relaxed at my presence.

James looked up too, eyes switching between Will, me, coming back to rest on Luca, before deciding against it and looking at the ground.

"What's he doing here?" James asked, motioning towards Will, who smiled a little.

"Savin' you lot from utter boredom at the 'ands of this dreadful day."

James nodded, "Okay, then, what do you suggest we do to tame the boredom?"

Will shrugged, "Well, I was thinkin' we could pop open a bottle of whiskey and trapes around town, eh?"

I glanced at him for a second, trying to tell if he was serious.

The smirk on his face said he wasn't.

James just shook his head, "No."

"Well, I don't see you comin' up with any better ideas, or frankly, any ideas for that matter."

Luca's brows knit together in confusion, his eyes darting back and forth, telling me he was trying to understand exactly where the conversation was going from the few words he could understand.

I didn't have time to translate for him, I was too worried about trying to translate for myself. My mind was cloudy as it was after Will's actions in the entryway, but all this English, along with Will's accent thrown in was making it impossible to understand a word of the conversation.

"Okay, I'll come up with an idea then, uh, Hide-and-Seek."

Will snorted, "That is 'onestly the worst thing that 'as come out of your mouth in the two years you've been 'ere, James."

"Well, it's better than going bottoms up on some cheap whiskey you brought."

"Who said it was gonna be *my* whiskey?"

A pause, which was helpful. I was still stuck on 'Hide

and seek.'

Hide and seek.

Nascondere.

Hide.

E.

And.

Cercare.

Seek.

Wait...

Nascondino.

Hide-and-Seek.

Oh, yeah, that was stupid.

We weren't *ragazzi,* children, anymore.

"Well, I say we put it to a vote."

Will scoffed, "James, we ain't parliament."

"And we *ain't* drinking whiskey."

"Fine."

Both of them turned to me for my reply first.

Though *Nascondino* was incredibly childish, there wasn't much else to do, so I shrugged.

"Sure. Anything to get out of this house."

James looked at me, "Oh, no we're not doing it outside."

"There are only so many places we can hide around the house, James," I said, a little annoyed, "Besides the woods and the field would make great hiding places."

"But it's raining."

I glanced out the window, it was only drizzling a little, the heavy rain had come and gone earlier in the day.

"A little water never hurt anyone," I said.

"Well, see what Luca thinks about it."

I nodded before turning to an overly confused Luca.

"You want to play *Nascondino?*"

Luca's eyes brightened a little. We used to play a lot

when we were younger, the vineyard was always the best place for it. Luca, Marco, a few other kids, and I would spend hours in that vineyard hiding from each other.

It brought back memories of better times. Back when we didn't understand what freedom was, and why we didn't have it. When soldiers would smile at us as we passed in the streets, who'd let us try on their caps and tell us about the medals on their chest. When we got older, the same soldiers sneered at us, thinking we would pull guns on them and proclaim *Italia's* freedom.

They weren't exactly wrong about that.

Luca nodded, "*Si.*"

I turned back to Will and James, "He wants to."

I looked at Will, almost pleadingly to say yes.

He huffed, "Fine, yes, let's play 'Ide-and-Seek. Anythin' to get you lot out of this 'ouse."

"Who's gonna find the rest of us?" James asked.

I shrugged, "Does anyone want to?"

Will shook his head, and so did James. I voiced my displeasure at being the one trying to find everyone as well, which left Luca, who looked at us before blinking a second, and locking eyes with me.

"*Io il cercatore, no?*" he said, letting out a sigh.

I'm the seeker, aren't I?

I smirked a little at his reaction, "*Si. Conto fino a trenta.*"

"Okay," he turned around, "*Uno, due, tre, quattro, cinque, sei-*"

The three of us not counting spun around, making a break for the door. James got there first, throwing the wooden door open. I was about to take the lead, but Will gripped my hand as we moved and pulled me back, making my cheeks flare up as he pulled us out the door.

The trees had started to turn yellow and red, though there was still some green thrown in the mix. I couldn't help marveling at how full the trees were here, and how beautiful the forest was.

It had slowly stopped raining as we ran deeper and deeper into the forest trying to get as far away from Luca as possible. Will's hand was still holding mine as we trapsed through the woods.

I slowed down to admire how the forest looked as the early morning fog had started to clear and small rays of light broke through the leaves, casting a blotchy pattern on the ground. There were still drops of rain falling through the trees, but they were quite small and only a few would land on my skin.

Will stopped after noticing my fascination with our surroundings so that I could look around.

We were in a clearing. Wild flowers sprinkled the grass while tree branches covered the small space. Will and I both sat down, and I reached down to pluck a small daisy from the dirt, twirling it around between my thumb and forefinger.

"Think we should be alright 'ere," Will said, letting out a breath.

My eyes shifted from the flower, over to him.

"You think they'll be able to find us?"

Will laughed a little before inching closer to me, "Maybe."

And then we fell silent, marveling at the serenity of the clearing.

The wind rustled the leaves in the trees as I took a moment to enjoy the peace. I wasn't running, I wasn't hiding, I-

I didn't have my gun.

I forgot my gun.

Merda.

And in that moment, in the middle of that open spot of land, my mind went blank, and all I could think about was I was in an unprotected, open space without a gun.

"Mara?" Will said, though his voice sounded as if I was hearing it through church glass.

I knew my hands were starting to shake and my breath was getting caught in my throat. I was having trouble breathing. I was trying to hide both my shaky breath, and trembling hands, and it wasn't working. I needed something to stop me from thinking about how this would be a great place for an ambush. My shoulder was stinging, the old gunshot wound finding its own way to haunt me, making me remember the last time I was ambushed.

I needed to calm down. I needed to stop. I couldn't have an attack with Will. He couldn't see how messed up I was. Because if he even got a hint of it, he'd run. The full story, he'd disappear into thin air.

No John I'd ever heard of fancied someone whose head was messed up.

"Mara, you alright?"

My attention snapped away from my racing mind, and towards Will, whose eyes were laced with concern.

"Yes, I'm alright," I said, lying.

I paused, trying to ignore the raging fear inside me.

I could get shot here.

Even if I knew there was no one trying to shoot me, the thought still crept into the back of my mind.

I looked at Will, "You haven't told me a lot about your life here," I said, needing to talk about something to get my thoughts away from my vulnerability.

He smiled at me, "Well, what do you want to know?"

A lot.

I felt like I needed to know everything about Will. I hadn't even felt this way about Marco, whom I'd known my whole life. I didn't think I could feel this way about a person who I barely knew.

"As much as you can tell me."

The smile on his face grew, and his eyes sparkled in the sunlight, "Alright," he said.

He leaned back, lying down on the grass before motioning for me to join him. I had to stifle a laugh as I let my back rest on the soft ground, the green blades tickling the exposed parts of my neck and legs. My long pants and white collared shirt became damp as I laid on the dewy ground. I exhaled, before I felt a warm hand intertwine with mine. My eyes snapped to the person next to me. Will was looking up at the sky as if nothing happened, and his expression still didn't change as he took our intertwined hands and placed them over his chest, subconsciously pulling us closer.

My heart was speeding up, chugging along like a steam engine going faster than it should. I couldn't tell if it was Will's hand in mine, and how I could feel the beating of his own chest under my palm, or how vulnerable I was without my gun on me.

"Well, I was born in London, lived there for the first few years of my life, can't remember much other than a few alleyways. But then my parents, can't remember much of them either, dropped me and my brother, Peter, off with my grandpa 'ere in Falmouth. We never 'eard from 'em again. We 'elped 'im with the doctor business, gettin' supplies, 'elpin' with bandages, all those things. My brother was always good at it, 'ad a gift for it. So did I.

Then England went to war, and 'e enlisted as an army doc. 'Is first time seein' action, 'e was in a medical tent when a bomb dropped on 'em, and well..." He drifted off as he took the hand that wasn't holding mine, and held it above both of us, making a gesture alluding to an explosion.

"*Merda*," I muttered, not really sure what else to say.

Luca hadn't known what to say to me when my parents died and now I understood why.

It was hard to say something.

What the hell could I say?

I hated people telling me sorry, because it wasn't their fault and I hated the phrase 'they're in a better place,' because I knew that there was no such thing as a heaven. Those were the two things people said because they couldn't think of anything else to say. I hadn't been entirely sure when it happened that I wanted them to say something. So with the realization about Will's brother, I didn't say anything. I just gave his hand a squeeze.

He smiled at me gratefully, as if he was tired of hearing empty words himself.

"I kept workin' with Grandpa. It didn't take me long without my brother doin' all the important stuff, like stitches and settin' broken bones, to figure out I wanted to do that for the rest of my life. When the war ends, I'm 'opin' I can go to the medical school in London, learn a few tricks, and 'ave a practice like Grandpa's back there. Figure more people need a doctor that doesn't ask questions there than 'ere."

I blinked, "That's true."

"Yeah," he let out a breath. With the rise and fall of his chest, our hands moved up and down as well, "And now, I'm 'ere, in a field, playin' 'Ide-and-Seek with a beautiful Italian girl, her friend, and the guy who all 'e does is sell papers."

I laughed a little, finally starting to feel my panic leave my body, "And is that a good thing or a bad thing?"

His black hair fell to the side and he winked, "'Aven't decided yet, Mara."

"Really?"

"Really."

A pause for a second as a breeze swept across us, and then I looked back at Will.

"Thanks for telling me."

He shrugged, "Yeah, it was only fair, I mean, I feel like I know so much about you already."

I smirked, "You don't even know half of it."

"Oh? And what about you do I not know?"

I couldn't help but wink, "All in due time."

"Ah, a mystery," he said, a smirk creeping onto his face.

"It appears so."

I blinked, wondering how long we'd been out here. Where the hell were Luca and James?

Did Luca get lost?

High probability.

Had he found James yet?

Who knew.

I turned over, lying on my side, facing Will, who did the same. He released my hand, making me already miss the warmth.

"How long do you think it'll take for them to find us?"

He blinked, before his eyes flickered to my lips, and it felt like he'd gotten closer to me.

"'Opefully a few hours," Will replied, as if his mind was elsewhere.

"Wha-"

And then his lips pressed into mine, making me lose

my balance. I fell on my back, taking Will down with me. I gasped at the impact of the ground, and he pulled away for a second, laughing a little at the circumstances of the fall.

I laughed. I had no idea why I found the whole thing funny myself.

"What was that for?" I asked, and I realized why I was laughing.

This whole kissing thing was different to me. It didn't exactly feel weird, it felt, well, new.

Sure, I'd kissed Marco, but nothing like this. Nothing spontaneous, and nothing that made my heart race this fast.

I was laughing at the idea that perhaps I enjoyed kissing Will.

Well, no perhaps. I *did* enjoy kissing Will.

And you're just figuring this out now?

In my defense, I've been a little too busy translating everything that's being said to me and others to consider how I feel about being kissed.

Right.

Will smirked, his body was situated over mine, and his hands were on either side of my face, keeping him from crashing right into me. His hair hung down, and I couldn't help but reach up and brush it aside as he talked, "Well, we're alone in a beautiful clearin', with no interruptions, I say we make the most of it."

I raised an eyebrow, "You do?"

He bit his lip, placing a hand on my cheek, "Yeah."

I smiled, laughing a little, maybe out of nervousness, or maybe I was just really happy.

I was in a beautiful country, away from war, where my own country's problems couldn't touch me, with a person who made my day better.

If I wasn't happy, there would have been something wrong with me.

And in that moment, I wasn't worried about not having my gun, I wasn't thinking about where the hell Luca was, or what the hell was happening with the Resistance, or if we were winning or losing the war.

I was thinking about how Will was looking down at me, and how safe I felt with him.

"Alright then. Let's make the most of it, shall we?" I said with a smile.

Will leaned down closer to my lips, his breath hitting them, before he moved to the side slightly to whisper in my ear.

"We shall."

And then his lips connected with mine.

And I was happy.

CHAPTER 15

**October 15th, 1943, 10:56am, Falmouth,
Cornwall, England
James**

The fallen leaves on the ground crunched against my feet as I raced through the trees, trying to outrun my pursuer.

I should've hidden farther into the woods.

Luca had found me in what seemed like the first minute, and I had done the only rational thing: run. But now my side ached and my breathing labored, and looking back, running was not the rational decision.

I glanced behind me, seeing Luca a few yards back. He was getting closer.

I smiled at how childish this was, playing Hide-and-Seek like I used to do when my parents and I came down to visit Uncle before the war. But this was fun, even if my whole body was telling me that I shouldn't be running.

I turned my attention forward again, feeling the need to pay attention, but it was too late, or just in time, because I found myself centimeters away from colliding with a tree.

I blinked once, letting out a labored breath. A hand circled around my wrist and spun me around, and my eyes locked on the hazel ones that always seemed to pull my focus.

Luca smirked, "Found you," he said in English. He was getting better. His accent was still thick, but I could understand.

"You did," I couldn't help but laugh at the boyish look on his face. A sense of pride that he was able to actually catch one of the three people hidden in the forest. It was a cute face. I still felt his grasp on my wrist, and couldn't help looking down at it, before my eyes snapped back up at him as if asking if he really wanted to keep doing that.

He glanced at his hand, and almost as if he had touched an open flame, he pulled it away.

Silence as I watched Luca put his side against the large tree I'd almost run into, and I copied his movements, picking at a loose piece of bark between us. I looked up at the trees and blinked.

"How do you say tree?" I asked, pointing at the thing we were leaning on.

He smiled, a smile that made my stomach do flip flops.

He had a great smile.

It was always crooked, I noticed. The detail made me grin a little as well.

"*Albero.*"

I liked the way he said it, the way it rolled off his tongue.

I wanted to hear him speak more, so I looked for something else, finding a stick close to my foot, picking it up.

"Stick?"

"*Bastone.*"

I picked up a leaf, "Leaf?"

He chuckled.

Was I bothering him?

I straightened and let the leaf plummet to the ground, thinking he wasn't going to translate. As if he thought this game of ours was more childish than Hide-and-Seek.

"*Foglia,*" he said, some sort of teasing tinged his voice. His voice in Italian, it might have been on purpose, but it was velvet, deep, melodic.

Beautiful.

And in that moment, I knew I fancied him.

It could have been the worst mistake of my life, but I did. The way I felt when I was around him, how I wanted to learn everything about this person in front of me. How I studied him differently than everyone else. How when we'd touch, it felt like electricity was being sent in waves up my arm. How I was drawn to him in ways I couldn't explain.

"How do you say, uh," I held up my hands making a heart, and having it float around my head like they did in the comics.

Luca blinked for a second, unsure what I was trying to do. If I was being perfectly honest, I didn't know either.

"*Amore,*" he said, barely a whisper on his tongue.

A warm breeze passed us and it made his un-pomaded hair get swept to the side.

"Uh, again?" I asked, my mouth all of a sudden dry.

I watched as his cheeks started to get a crimson tint to them, and he looked down for a second, as if gathering his thoughts. When he looked up, I wasn't looking at his eyes anymore, I was looking at his mouth.

"*Amore.*"

If it was even possible, his voice got quieter, and I suddenly became aware of how close we actually were.

Now, I was looking at his lips, wondering what it'd be like to close the gap between us.

I'd never kissed someone before.

But I was sure that kiss would be great.

"How do you uh, how do you say..." I trailed off as I brought my two hands up, putting the fingertips of each hand together so they looked like shadow puppet people, and then touched the hands together. "Kiss," I said, my breath shaky. I found myself fearful of what would happen next.

Luca blinked. He blinked again. There was a look in his eyes, but I couldn't tell if it was panic, or something else.

The silence dragged on a little too long, and so I let out a breath, I myself panicking.

Why the hell would I say that?

"You know what, forge-"

"*Bacio.*"

I barely heard him, his voice not even a whisper.

"Bacio?" I said, trying to get the accent right.

"*Bacio.*"

The word sent a shiver down my spine as my eyes kept shifting from his hazel ones, to his lips, to a leaf on the ground.

But no matter how hard I tried to focus on the odd orange color of the leaf, all I could think about was how much I wanted to *bacio* him.

Getting a well of courage I didn't know I had, I moved closer, just a small bit, just a little, but he didn't move, instead looking down. I raised my hand to his cheek, which got him to tilt his head back up towards me.

"*Bacio*," I muttered, almost to myself, before I moved even closer, and that second, I did the one thing I really, really, wanted to do.

I kissed him.

And then the courage was gone, and I pulled away, as if his lips were on fire.

Bloody hell why did I do that?

I watched as Luca's eyes widened, taken back by my action. I was panicking.

I shouldn't have done that.

Words caught in my throat as I fought to say something, anything to the Italian boy in front of me.

The Italian *boy* I had just kissed.

I backed away, almost tripping on a twig, "I, I'm, I, I shouldn't, I shouldn't have done that, I'm sorry, I thought, I just, bloody hell that was a mistake, I should, I should go," I started to turn around, trying to leave the mess behind me, but a warm hand grabbed my arm and spun me around, pulling me back towards the tree.

Luca's hazel eyes held me to the spot as his gaze shifted towards my mouth, and then back up to my eyes. I opened my mouth to speak, but I didn't know exactly what the bloody hell to say.

Instead, he spoke, "*Si, bacio*," his voice was quivering, and I could see how his eyes darted around, nervous. Scared even.

And then, he took an uneven breath and leaned forward ever so slightly, our noses almost touching. My eyes closed, but then opened again, afraid I'd miss this time.

Luca's eyes were closed, one arm trying to hold himself up against the tree, the other still on my arm, in a sort of death grip. And the way his hand felt like it was shaking, told me he was nervous.

I took a breath, before finally, I leaned forward ever so slightly and pressed my lips to his once again. This time, I didn't pull away. It was soft at first, hesitant, but as I felt his lips start to move with mine, I cupped his face in my hands, pulling him closer.

There were sparks of electricity everywhere. In the air around us and in his arms as they wrapped around my neck.

And suddenly, something that had moments ago felt like the biggest mistake of my life, now felt like the best thing I'd ever done.

I moved my hands from his face, down to his waist and pulled him closer, if that was even possible.

I didn't want to pull away, because I knew that once I did, we'd be back in the real world. Two boys. Kissing. That reality would be too much for the both of us.

So I just held on to him, kissing him, holding him in my arms.

And I never wanted to let him go.

I broke away, but not by much. Our lips brushed as we tried to get some sort of air.

I inhaled, "I think you found me."

Luca

Ci stavamo baciando
We were kissing.
I was in his arms.
He was holding me.
My arms were wrapped around his neck.
My back was being pressed against the rough bark of the tree, digging into my shirt.
It was perfect.
This was perfect.
One of his hands ran up my torso and stopped where the three buttons on my shirt were undone, and I felt him pull me closer to him, gripping me tight.

And then his other hand snaked under my shirt in the back. I let out a gasp as his cold hands hit my skin, he smiled into my lips at the reaction.

This was incredible.

James had kissed me, and now I was kissing back.

Wait.

James was kissing me.

He was kissing *me.* Another *he.*

My eyes snapped open.

No.

Merda.

I was kissing a boy.

No.

My stomach, that two seconds ago was doing flip flops at how his ocean eyes drowned me, was now filling with bile.

No.

Fanculo, no.

This wasn't happening.

I wasn't breathing.

My lips were still on his.

His hands were still on me.

My arms were still around him.

I pulled away.

James looked at me, his eyes filled with concern, "Luca, are you-"

"No."

"What?"

"This, no, I, I can't."

"What? Luca, why?"

I blinked.

Perche?

So many reasons.

So many reasons why this was bad.

So many times I'd been told this, what had just happened, was wrong.

This wasn't supposed to happen.

I shouldn't have let it happen.

I shouldn't have pulled him back.

I should have just let him leave when he tried.

"I can't. This is not good," I tried to get out, trying to translate my panic.

I just kissed a boy.

Fanculo.

"To kiss?"

Did he not get it?

"For two, two, men, to kiss, James."

James's blue eyes paralyzed me as they softened, "Luca-"

I shook my head and closed my eyes, breaking contact with him. I tried to push him off me in a frenzy. But through my flailing limbs he still held onto me, trying to keep me still, trying to calm me down.

He was a newsboy, I was a farm hand.

I was stronger.

I pushed him harder this time, and he loosened his grip long enough for me to run. I didn't know where I was going, I didn't know how I got here, but I needed to run away from him.

From what just happened.

From how I liked it.

"Luca, wait-"

But I didn't hear the rest.

I didn't *want* to hear the rest.

I just wanted to disappear.

I kissed a boy.

It was wrong.

It wasn't right.

And it felt good.

Il diavolo must have been having a real nice time playing with me.

I tripped over a tree root, stumbling to the ground, but got up and kept going. I was running as fast as I possibly could away from this situation. Away from what I had done. But James was charming, he was kind, he was amazing.

But none of those things justified what I did, because he was a *him.*

I broke through the trees, sprinting onto the field, running faster than I had run away from the ENR soldiers.

The scene of James's lips on mine persisted in my mind.

The way he held me, the way he looked at me, the way his hands felt against my skin. It kept replaying over and over in my head.

It wouldn't stop. The feeling wouldn't go away.

I found myself at the front of the house quicker than I expected. I didn't even bother to knock, I knew Mr. Smithson wouldn't be home.

I blew through the entryway, racing up the stairs to my room, but I stopped right before the door. It was James's room too.

I wanted to lock myself somewhere where I couldn't be reminded of my mistake. So I turned around and walked into Mara's room. It was clean. Everything packed away, except for a hairbrush on her dresser and some lipstick that looked to be five years old. I couldn't help but collapse as soon as I got within two feet of her bed, though I winced a little as I felt my head hit something hard under the pillow.

I lifted my head up, before pulling her gun out from under the thing.

Merda, she didn't have it on her.

She must have been doing a lot better than I was if she was leaving her gun behind.

I looked up at the ceiling, tears pricking the corners of my eyes.

I wasn't crying because of what I'd done. I was crying because no matter how wrong it was, no matter how horrible the priests had made it sound, no matter how much of a sin it was, I couldn't deny how right it felt.

It felt amazing.

I didn't understand it, nor was I sure I wanted to.

So I laid there, tears rolling down my face, because I wanted something that I not only couldn't want, but could never, ever have.

CHAPTER 16

October 28th, 1943, 5:23pm, Falmouth,
Cornwall, England
Mara

Sweat was covering my face. Why did I have to do this again?

Right. Because for some reason Luca was busy working the ticket booth, even though Mr. Smithson had it covered, and James was selling papers. Something that he had all of a sudden started doing again. He'd been helping Luca with the projects that Mr. Smithson straight up refused to let me do. Until all of a sudden, that stopped. And I was having to pick up the slack.

Culo pigro.

I finished the last shovel full of coal, chucked it into the train, and gave the conductor a salute to tell him I was finished.

It was the last train of the night, and I was exhausted. The trains had been relentless all day, and I barely had enough time to breathe.

My shoulders ached as I drove the shovel into the coal I was standing on top of, before hopping down. My legs wobbled a little with the impact of solid ground compared to the shakiness of the coal. I got used to the feeling though, and brushed my hands on my pants.

The sun was going down in the distance, which was

usually Mr. Smithsons cue to start packing up. I watched as James started to put the leftover newspapers into his messenger bag. He'd probably keep them for the next day in case anyone missed out on the news.

I didn't exactly get chances to talk to James these days. Luca and I were always talking by ourselves, and I'd been trying to teach him more English.

Whenever I asked James to join us, or whenever it was the three of us alone, James would go the other direction. The same could be said for Luca. I tried to ask about it once, but Luca just told me I wouldn't understand, so I let it go. He'd tell me when he wanted to. Though I didn't know how long that would take.

I hurried over to Luca, not wanting to get in a discussion with James. Since Luca wasn't talking to him anymore, James had tried to strike up a conversation or two with me. I wasn't exactly the most talkative person in the world, so I was trying to avoid him as best I could.

What time I wasn't spending with Luca, trying to keep him company, I was spending with Will, who had been showing me around Falmouth. The rocky cliffs, the beautiful shoreline, the quiet town center. We'd been talking, trying to get to know each other more, and walking, and well, kissing. It made me subconsciously smile at the thought.

Luca gave me a nod when I reached him.

"How was business today?" I asked.

"Well, everyone could understand me, so I'd say not bad."

I couldn't help smirk, "Now we just have to work on that accent of yours."

"It's mysterious."

"It's a giveaway. If someone asks you where you're from

what're you going to say, huh? 'Oh, you know, Italy, the country currently still halfway loyal to fascism and Hitler.' Yeah, I don't think so. And you're a horrible liar."

"Am not."

I raised an eyebrow, "May I remind you of those poker games you tried to bluff in?"

That was another thing we'd been doing. Playing poker. James didn't know how to play, so for some reason, Luca had always insisted on that being the card game of choice. Even when I'd suggested that James could watch us play to learn how to, the blonde would refuse.

It made me really want to know why exactly they were avoiding each other if it was bad enough they couldn't be in the same room together.

Did Luca tell him he looked like a Nazi?

Damn it if he did. I told him to not point that out. Supposedly that was a touchy subject.

"Whatever. How was shoveling?"

I scoffed, "You mean, throwing pounds upon pounds of rocks up into a coal car of a train without any help? Almost as bad as moving that *dannato* plow by myself."

As if my body decided that was its cue, my arms screamed at me as I stuffed my hands into the pockets of my khaki pants.

"Well, sorry, I had my own job to do," Luca said, amusement seeping from his voice.

"Yeah, the age old excuse."

He used to say things like that when he didn't want to do any of the heavy lifting at the farm. 'Oh, I need to cut the grapes,' 'Oh, I have to go feed *i maiali*, the pigs,' the list went on and on.

Mr. Smithson came out of the booth, locking the door behind him before motioning for us to follow him to the carriage.

The silence once we were on the road could only be described as the most awkward experience ever, as it had been for the last few weeks. I didn't talk because I felt like I already said every possible thing those first few days trying to spark a conversation. At this point I'd just given up and let silence engulf the three of us.

Mr. Smithson was oblivious to the change. He was going on about some woman who kept wanting to change her ticket to get her back to London, which wasn't possible. No trains were running *to* London, they were only going away from it.

He droned on and on, despite being ignored by the three of us in the back.

I shifted, moving my leg like a metronome, back and forth, and tapping my hand on the wood. Anything to make the silence less, well, silent. But it didn't work. I looked between Luca and James. *Mi fratello* was looking down at a loose board, and James was trying to pay attention to the rolling fields to the side of us. I thought his transfiction was odd, seeing how he'd seen the fields thousands of times. However, every so often I noticed his blue eyes moving from the grass to Luca, trying to read him.

I felt like telling him that was a lost cause.

No matter how well me and Luca knew each other, if one of us didn't want anyone to know what we were thinking, or what we were feeling, no one would know. We had become good at hiding feelings.

Perhaps me more than Luca.

I couldn't bear the silence anymore, needing some sort of conversation, so I gathered my thoughts, and huffed, looking at James.

"How was business?"

James's head snapped over to me, and even Luca looked up, eyeing the blonde carefully.

James cleared his throat, "Good, fine, yeah, it was good," he said, stumbling over his words.

He never held eye contact with me, his gaze kept flickering over to Luca, who was situated beside me.

We fell silent once again.

Damn these two.

"And?" I pried.

"And what?" James said.

He tried to sound nonchalant, but instead came across as if he was in some sort of interrogation.

"You have any stories?"

"Oh, uh, well, yes, one guy was passing through, about our age actually, visiting his sick grandmother in Liverpool. Gave me a pound for the paper."

Luca's gaze shifted up. It was almost as if James knew it would, because as soon as Luca looked up, their eyes locked.

"Why would he do that?" Luca asked through his teeth.

His English was definitely getting better.

James blinked, "Said I had a charming smile," his voice was low and serious, his eyes looked directly at Luca, as if challenging him. To what, I had no idea.

Maybe Luca had insulted his smile.

I wouldn't have pegged James for being that vain, but it was possible.

We fell into silence again. But this time, both Luca and James kept sneaking glances at each other.

When we finally came to a stop in front of the house, it seemed as though it had been hours. So much so that I practically leapt out of the carriage and ran into the house.

Mrs. Smithson was waiting in the parlor, knitting a scarf. She'd started about a week ago, saying that it was the new blanket.

'The soldiers need scarves, not blankets.' she'd said, 'They don't have time to sleep.'

Oh wow... What a thought... Who else would ever have suggested that those soldiers were too busy trying not to get blown up to sleep?

Perhaps it was me?

But who knew.

It was her second scarf she'd knit, and it made me wonder if she had anything else to do with her life besides try to feel like she was a part of something bigger than herself, when really, she was just trying to feel good about herself. That's what I'd figured out early on about these women who made blankets and sent food to the troops. It wasn't for the soldiers, it was for them to talk about how much they'd helped.

When I walked into the parlor, I sat down and started to shuffle the deck of cards, as I knew that's what Luca would want to do as soon as he got in the house. Mrs. Smithson looked up at me and set her needles down, sliding a worn and dirty envelope across the wood coffee table between us.

"What is that?" I asked.

"Letter. Didn't say from where."

I grabbed the envelope from the table quickly.

If it didn't say from where, I knew exactly where it was from. It'd just been smuggled through several illegal checkpoints to get here.

Ripping open the letter, I carefully unfolded the dusty paper. It was covered in gunpowder, and dust. Along the edges and dotted around the page was a faded crimson. In some places it would mix with the ink.

Blood.

The handwriting was messy, but legible, and in *Italiano.* I took a deep breath before reading it. Afraid of the contents, I prepared myself for the worst.

It'd all been in vain.

The Axis powers got to us.

La Resistenza had fallen.

I'd been checking the papers. Anything to do with Italy had been discussing *Roma* and the Jewish population there. Nothing of *Napoli* and nothing of *la Resistenza.* Only the Allies and the *Nazisti.*

Just read the dannata thing already.

One more deep breath before I let my eyes run back and forth across the page.

Mara,

I hope you are well in England and the people there are treating you well. I bring news of la Resistenza. We were able to take Napoli, after four days. Thanks to you and Luca's supply runs, we were able to give civilians protection against the Nazisti. The Allies are in Napoli now, and we've moved on to Roma where several other groups are gathering, and hope to be joined by the Allied troops soon.

I was waiting for the but. There always a but with Filomina. Especially when she started out with good news. I held my breath as I read on.

However. I don't just bring news of happiness. It is with a heavy heart that I have to be the one to tell you this. The man who escorted you to safety, Marco, is dead. Though, he died fighting for us. He told me he'd talked with a very persuasive girl about freedom, and remembered what he wanted to fight for to begin with. I am sorry for your loss, Mara. He is

in a better place without this war tormenting him.
I hope all is well there,
Filomina

A ringing pierced my ears as I read the letter over again.

The breath was knocked out of me.

I couldn't think straight.

Marco died fighting for freedom. He died for what was right.

The one time that he'd been trying to do good, they ripped it away from him.

The same soldiers who'd probably fought by him at one time killed him because he was fighting for a safer country. A free country.

I felt sick to my stomach. My mind raced, trying to search for answers, trying to figure out how this could possibly happen.

I was going to throw up.

Maybe if I had been there, I could have covered for him. I could have helped him.

I could have saved him.

"Mara, is everything okay? You look pale," Mrs. Smithson asked.

I nodded, "Fine."

But I wasn't.

My best friend just died.

Someone I had loved once. Someone I imagined a future with.

I felt like someone had just cut out a chunk of my heart.

Even if I didn't love him now, even if I had feelings for someone else. I had still shared most of my life with him.

If he'd lived, he could've gone on to fight in *la Resistenza*. He could have gone on to help free *Italia*. Just like he'd always wanted. But now, he was just another corpse.

Another tally marker to the constantly growing number of casualties I'd seen in the papers. And that hurt.

I wanted to scream.

I wanted to punch something.

I wanted to shoot something.

But I couldn't. Mrs. Smithson was right there. And she was watching me closely, her brows knit closely together, assessing me.

I needed to get out of there.

"Excuse me," I said, not really understanding why I would excuse myself.

The letter was clutched in my palm so tightly I was afraid it was going to turn to dust. My heart pounded, and I could hear the blood pumping in my ears.

I got to my room and closed the door, locking it behind me.

I needed my gun.

I hadn't been carrying it for the past few weeks because I hadn't needed it. I'd felt safe.

Now, with Marco dead, I felt like I was next on some cosmic hit list and all of a sudden, my mind told me I needed a gun. I needed to protect myself.

I wasn't there to protect Marco. So I needed to protect myself. I grabbed the gun from under my pillow, and tucked it into my waistband, making me let out a sigh of relief.

I wobbled a little on my feet.

This wasn't happening.

Marco couldn't be dead.

But he was.

Filomina never lied.

An image of Marco's body on the ground flooded my vision. His normally groomed hair, messy and matted with blood. His green eyes, the ones that were so rare among *Italiani*, the ones that I'd always used to dream about, looked cloudy, and his lips parted slightly as if in the middle of saying his last words. One hand would have been under a gun, probably the one his own father had given him at around the same time as I'd received mine. The other, draped across his chest. His coat would be covered in blood. Not just his, but the blood of the corpses around him.

I fell onto my bed, my legs unable to support the weight of the truth.

I couldn't help myself from letting my eyes blur with tears.

He hadn't just been a person I loved. He'd been my best friend. He was closer to me than Luca was in many ways. He had been the one I'd told my secrets to first before I trusted Luca enough to tell him.

Luca.

Merda, this would crush him.

Luca dealt with people dying a lot harder than me. I'd seen people take their last breath too many times. This was one of the only deaths in the world that could get me to cry. Luca had only seen one or two people die, he would be more of a mess than me.

Tears flowed freely down my face as I read the letter again.

He's in a better place without this war tormenting him.

Dio, I hoped Filomina was right. I really, really did.

I looked over at the window. The sun was going down and a beautiful sunset was painted across the sky. If there really was such a thing as heaven, I imagined Marco made that sunset as a way to comfort me. Telling me everything was going to be fine.

Even if it wasn't.

No one would give him a funeral, they'd just burn him with the rest of the corpses like they always did. Perhaps the Allies would be more respectful, but I doubted it. No matter what side they were on, armies didn't care about casualties that weren't their own, nor did they want to.

I got up from my bed, wiping the tears from my face that refused to stop dripping down and made my way to the window. I threw it open and let the crisp autumn air hit my skin. This time, climbing down the ivy was easier. I'd done it a lot more since the first time, especially in the past few weeks when I went to go meet Will. It was a lot more fun that way.

My feet hit the ground and I took off towards the beach.

I didn't want to tell Luca, afraid if I did, he'd become more reserved than he already was. Though he had talked to me a lot lately, it felt like he was holding back, as if for the first time in our lives he wasn't telling me something. I didn't think that telling him our closest friend died would help with that.

Soon enough, my boots were sinking into sand, and the sound of the waves crashing onto the beach filled my ears. I looked out into the open expanse that was the ocean, and then looked up at the red and orange sky, tears brimming the corners of my eyes.

As much as I hated it, memories came rushing back. Long nights in the old vineyard, stolen kisses behind a pastry shop, getting drunk on New Years, learning to shoot our guns together.

My mind kept going back to how he looked at me. How his lips felt against mine. How he told me he loved me.

The last time I saw him at the train station. He'd told me the same thing, and I'd forgiven him. I was so close to letting what we had die. But I didn't. I forgave him. In my mind I'd thought it was a mistake to forgive someone who'd caused me so much pain. Now, I was grateful I'd done it while he was still breathing.

I'd told him he'd shattered me. That was nothing in comparison to what I was feeling now.

I huffed, pulled out my gun, and turned the safety off. I raised it above my head and my hand tightened on the trigger as I shot into the air. *La Resistenza's* traditional funeral. At least, it was before we started being hunted by the ENR.

BANG!

"*Ciao, Marco. Ti amero sempre.* I'll always love you," I whispered to no one in particular.

And it was true. Maybe not in the way I had before, when it had simply been the two of us in our small town. But I still did.

I blinked, feeling one last tear roll down my cheek, wondering where that bullet went.

Then I heard the sound of sand shifting under a boot and I spun around, gun raised, pointed at the person who followed me here.

But when I looked at the man in front of me, I practically threw the gun back into my waistband.

Fanculo.

Poliziotto.

The man stood with one hand on his own gun, and the other out in front of him. If this were any other circumstance, I would have laughed at the ridiculous hat on his head. But now, I felt like shrinking away from it.

"Miss, do you have a license for that gun?"

My mind was too focused on Marco to translate quickly, and I didn't respond fast enough. I was just staring at the *poliziotto* blankly.

"Miss?"

Then it clicked.

Merda, I didn't have a license.

People needed licenses for guns here?

"No," I said flatly, not wanting to risk saying the wrong words in an accent.

He huffed, "Alright then, Miss, I'm gonna need to give you a ticket and then we can go down to the station to get that gun processed and get you a temporary license. Do you have identification on you?"

Pause.

Translate.

Focus on him. Not Marco.

Not on how I wanted to reach for my gun. Just to hold for comfort. But no matter how hard I tried, I couldn't understand *identification.*

"Identification?" I asked.

"Yes, Miss. Do you have it?"

"No, sir."

Was that a bad thing?

He huffed, "You have to have identification somewhere, perhaps at your house?"

I translated faster.

I shook my head, "I'm sorry, sir, I don't have what you're talking about."

His hand tightened on his holster, and I took a step back.

"Miss, were you born in England?"

Merda, Merda, Merda, Merda.

I had no choice but to shake my head, "No."

"When did you arrive here?"

I couldn't lie.

I had no documentation.

Any immigration to England had been cut off from Italy, or any other country with my accent.

And my gun. That was Italian as well.

I had no choice.

"A month ago, officer."

He tensed, "And where did you so happen to come from a month ago, with a gun?"

I could've said Spain, but my accent wasn't Spanish. I knew it. I sounded like some spoofed Italian character in one of those cartoons.

I could see the look in his eye.

He knew.

He just wanted me to confirm it.

I shook my head, "I don't see the reason for this."

"Where did you come from?" he said, more forceful this time, his hands already reaching for the gun in his holster.

As soon as his hand touched his, I instinctively reached for my own.

He's going to kill you, you need to protect yourself.

But as soon as my hand hit the metal, the *poliziotto* snapped.

"Drop the weapon!" he yelled, pulling the pistol, pointing it straight at my heart.

I didn't hear his words.

I saw the gun.

I saw what Marco saw before he died.

I saw death.

And I grabbed the Beretta.

"I said drop the weapon, Blackshirt!"

I froze.

I'd heard the term before. I'd used it before. It was the

common name of the Fascist National Party's army. Mussolini's lap dogs. Known for the odd black uniforms they wore.

Never in my life, would I ever thought I would be associated with those horrible people, and in the shock, my grip on the gun in my hand slackened.

My gun, my fathers gun, dropped to the ground, sand seeping into the cracks.

The officer advanced, his gun still raised, aimed at my chest.

"I dropped my gun, you can drop yours."

You goddamn idiot.

If there was one thing I learned with ENR soldiers around all the time, it was to hold my tongue. I had forgotten what that was like. One month and I had already started to feel comfortable with the freedom to say what I wanted. Now was not the time to be comfortable.

"I'm not lowering my only protection anytime soon, Italian spy."

Protection.

Against what? More protection?

Or did he think that my gun was ten times worse than his?

"I am not a spy," I said sharply, even as I watched him pull out handcuffs.

Was that really necessary?

You're a spy, remember? You're cunning and evil.

My stomach churned with the idea that he grouped me with the same people who'd killed Marco and who'd devastated my country. But then again, we all were the same to outsiders. We all looked the same, all sounded the same, all came from the same place.

We were all spies to them.

Il poliziotto gripped my hand, wrenching it behind my back, and then the other. Both made me yelp a little at how harsh he was being.

"That's what you people all say."

You people.

My teeth ground against each other as the cold metal of the cuffs bit into my wrists.

"I'm going to get you down to the station. We'll be able to hand you off to London in the morning."

My hands clenched. He was going to throw me in jail.

I watched as he grabbed my gun off the ground and looked at it.

"A spy's gun," he muttered, completely fascinated by the Beretta.

I couldn't help myself, "Have you ever even seen a spy before?"

He pushed me forward, making me stumble through the sand, "I'm looking at one of the sinners now."

Oh great. Not only did he think I was working for Mussolini, he also was a *Dio* fearing Christian.

Fanculo, this was not good.

———————

They'd tossed me in one of the tiniest cells in the small jail. It was dark, the only light was streaming in from a slit in the wall. I wasn't quite sure how they considered that a window. The small sliver let a single strip of light flood into the room, and the eerie glow sent a shiver down my spine. I couldn't tell if that shiver was because of the dark, or because of the cold stone floor.

There wasn't enough room for a bed. Instead there was a pillow. Supposedly this was where they kept overnighters, not someone serving time.

I'd listened to *il poliziotto* detail how he caught me. Or as he liked to call me, 'That Italian bitch.' According to him, he was just out for a stroll, doing his rounds along the coast where the homes were, and he heard the gunshot down at the beach. Immediately he raced towards the noise, afraid someone had been hurt. Instead, he found me, 'the spy,' standing there with a gun pointed straight at him. He assumed the shot was to draw him out. After all, spies always knew where their enemies were. He then heroically overpowered me before forcing me into handcuffs and dragging me down to the station.

The worst part was they believed everything he said.

And that was how I found myself here. In one of the smallest spaces I'd been in for a while.

It was around the size of a closet, with concrete walls and floors. The door took up almost all of one wall, and was iron. A lot of effort for the tiny cell.

The light streaming in reminded me of something.

I heard voices coming from outside.

"I told the blackshirt, stand down, or I'll shoot," the officer from before said as he was walking past my cell, footsteps slowly fading away.

Stand down or I'll shoot.

Stai giu o sparo.

I shivered.

Stai giu o sparo.

I felt my heart rate start to go up as my mind repeated the same phrase over and over again. But instead of the officer's voice, it was the voice of a twenty-some year old Italian man that rang through my ears.

My mind went blank. A memory surfacing in flashes.

My knees had been tucked into my chest, and I was squished between a bunch of coats. I couldn't see much.

But I could hear everything.

The front door slammed open.

"Payment," the voice had said.

The ENR had thought we needed to pay them to be in our town.

It was only fair considering they were protecting us.

Protecting us my culo, I remember thinking to myself as I sat inside that closet like I had done every time they came. We'd heard about raids turning ugly and bodies being left in soldiers wake. I'd never thought it would happen to us.

Until it did.

"This is less than last time."

My breathing got shallower and faster as the words played in my ears.

"We don't have anymore to offer you," my father's voice said. He never sounded weak even when he was facing an armed ENR soldier. I heard footsteps on the ground, polished boots.

I saw the light streaming into the closet through the gaps in the wood.

"There's always more you can give to your country, isn't there?"

I remember footsteps hitting the floor as drawers opened in the kitchen, things being taken out, plates being dropped, glass breaking.

My hands trembled.

"The ENR and the *Partito Nazionale Fascista* are not my country. *Italia* is my country."

"Then you are a traitor."

Something else broke and my heart rate sped up even more.

"And you are a traitor to your people, *figlio*."

Mio padre had always been vocal about his disdain of Fascist Italy. Perhaps that was where I got it from. But then was not the time to be vocal.

I bit my tongue, trying to control my breathing, trying to get my mind away from the memory, trying to stop seeing everything over again. It wasn't working. I was alone. No one was going to save me from my mind.

The voices came back, louder this time, along with the realistic closet doors in front of my face. I tried closing my eyes, it didn't help, I could still see everything as if it were happening right in front of me.

"Don't call me *un figlio*, I am a soldier in the ENR. It's in your best interest to respect me."

"And it's in your best interest to get out of my house."

"Payment first."

I couldn't stop my mind from racing. I couldn't control it.

"You two are awfully old to not have a child, are you sure one's not tucked away anywhere?"

That was what set my father off.

I had just been able to peer through the cracks of the door to see what was happening.

My father had grabbed the gun that he kept under the kitchen table.

"*Stai gui o sparo. Stai gui o sparo.*"

My father hadn't.

"I fought for this country's democracy, you're fighting for it's enslavement."

A gun went off.

BANG!

My mother let out a cry.

What happened next was a blur in my head. Another gunshot, footsteps, a door closing, me walking out of a closet to see my parents' blood run over the white tile of the kitchen floor.

The scene kept replaying, and it felt like the concrete walls around me were closing in.

My hands shook, and when I sat on them, my whole body vibrated. My heart was beating alarmingly fast, and my breathing had run ragged.

All I could hear was the same sentence over and over again.

Stai gui o sparo.

Stai gui o sparo.

Stai gui o sparo.

CHAPTER 17

October 28th, 9:40pm, Falmouth Cornwall, England.

Luca

Mara had left me alone with him. She'd locked herself in her room and wouldn't answer when I knocked. So I had no choice but to sit in James and I's room, staring at a piece of paper, trying to figure out what to draw. Embracing the silence between the blonde and I. Neither of us wanted to go down stairs.

Mrs. Smithson was on some tirade about how the troops needed more warm clothes for the winter months, and I had a feeling even her husband was trying to avoid her. James and I had no intention of becoming Mrs. Smithson's new audience, or Mr. Smithson's excuse to leave.

And so, silence overtook the room.

This was pathetic.

I knew it was.

But I was afraid if I talked to James, I'd say something or do something I'd regret. My English was getting better, so I couldn't feign not understanding him. And after I kissed him, or he kissed me, or... I didn't know at this point, I was trying to put as much distance between us as possible.

What I did was wrong. And it, feeling right, was the way for Satan to tempt me.

Mara would have laughed if I'd said that to her.

But it was true.

I snuck another glance at James, his head in that book he was always reading. His eyes were narrowed in concentration, and I couldn't help my stomach from doing a flip as I watched the blue circles skim the pages.

He looked up, and I snatched my eyes away from him. It was the first time we'd made eye contact since we got to the house. The last time was in the carriage, after he'd told us about the person who gave him a pound for a piece of paper.

Said I had a charming smile.

It made my insides churn with the idea of someone else taking a notice to the smile, but it made me feel better that he hadn't noticed his eyes. The eyes that so easily drowned me.

I'd been trying to convince myself I didn't want James. That the kiss we shared was just an impulsive cry for attention from someone, anyone. That I never actually wanted it.

But every time I started to forget it, I'd remember how good his lips felt on mine.

His hand under my shirt.

How he made my heart race.

It felt right.

It was wrong.

The silence wrapped around the room, making some invisible tension run taunt.

This was pathetic. We weren't talking, and we were the only two people either of us could talk to at the moment.

Ding dong!

Both James and I shot up out of our beds at the noise of a potential new person in the house.

If it was Will, entering through the front door for a change, I was going to yell. Even if she was in the room next to me with the door locked, I needed Mara here. I needed to know I wasn't entirely alone with James. I wasn't going to let Will sweep her away for what felt like the hundredth time.

Though I wasn't going to deny that when she was with him, she seemed to forget about *Italia* and what we left behind, what we did in the fight for freedom.

James and I dashed downstairs, both needing something to break the overwhelming silence.

Mr. Smithson got to the door first and the two of us hung back, trying to not interrupt. When the older man opened the door, it wasn't Will who was standing there, instead a man in a uniform stood in the doorway.

I recognized the uniform. I recognized the ridiculous hat.

Poliziotto.

I tensed at the sight of him.

"Good evening officer, what brings you here at this hour?"

Mr. Smithson was older, but he still commanded a room, and compared to the officer, he was a giant.

"Uh, good evening sir, uh, well, you see..." the young officer drifted off.

"Spit it out, son."

"Well, we apprehended a criminal tonight on the shore, a spy, who claims she was staying at your house for the last month or so."

Mr. Smithson shook his head, "I'm afraid I don't know what you mean, there are no spies in my house."

I watched as another *poliziotto* stepped forward, he carried himself differently than the younger one, his shoulders were back, chin lifted. He looked as though he'd just received a medal.

"The Blackshirt in question claims her name is Mara, I found her on the beach with a gun, and when I attempted to take her in, she not only didn't have identification on her, but pointed her gun at me when I tried to take her peacefully."

"I'm sorry, what?"

Mara.

That was the only word I knew through the whirlwind of formalities.

What the hell did she do?

James tapped me on my shoulder, and when I ignored him, his hand gripped mine, and pulled me away from the entryway, into the parlor.

I raised my eyebrows at him as if asking what the hell was going on.

He pointed back out towards the entryway, "That man thinks Mara's a spy."

"Why?"

"She's Italian and doesn't have papers on her. You need to stay out of sight."

I blinked, understanding.

"What happened to her?" I whispered.

James shook his head, "I don't know, hold on."

I could hear the voices, but with all the terms the *poliziotto* was using, it was hard to translate.

"Rest assured sir, she will be given the proper treatment for deceiving you. Officials are on their way to take her to London for further questioning."

I glanced over at Mr. Smithson, who started to get red in the face. But from this distance away, I couldn't tell if it was anger, or embarrassment.

James turned back to me, "Mara's in jail," his tone serious.

Mara had taught me that word a long time ago back in *Italia* when she'd learned it. She'd liked the sound of the word and how it rolled off her tongue.

I pieced his words together.

And my mind went blank.

Jail.

Mara was in jail.

She was in a confined space.

Merda.

I looked at James, a sheer look of panic on my face, "She can't be in jail, James, she doesn't do well in confined spaces, she, she, she *panico.*"

He nodded, "I know, Luca, I know."

"She can't-"

James's hand placed itself on my shoulder across from him. My eyes snapped to his.

"She's going to be fine, Luca."

"But-"

His grip tightened on my shoulder for a second before releasing it, "She's going to be okay."

I nodded, trying to focus my attention back on the discussion, hoping that Mr. Smithson could get her out.

The man in question looked like he was about to combust, "Officer, Mara is not a spy-"

"That's what you might think, sir, but these people are very good at tricking-"

"Officer, Mara was fleeing her country."

"Then why does she have a gun on her?"

Mr. Smithson blinked, he didn't know about the gun. I waited for him to question her motives. I waited for him to question our purpose here.

But that time never came.

Mr. Smithson kept a straight face as he spoke to the officer, but I saw his fists clench at his sides.

"She's a part of the Italian Resistance, you bloke. She's got a gun on her because she just crossed a hostile country, through Spain, and through international waters as a person who hates the country she comes from."

"Well, given the circumstances-"

"Given the circumstances, I'd assume you put a gun to her?"

"Yes, but-"

James stepped out from the parlor, leaving me alone to watch the scene play out before me.

He glanced back at me, nodding a little, before turning to the *poliziotto*, "Officer, this girl has stared down hostile guns for the past year. Do you think her first reaction was always to put her hands up?"

The officer looked at him, blinking, he was speechless as Mr. Smithson stepped in.

"Mara is no spy, officer. I assure you of that much, and I would greatly encourage her release immediately."

The officer shrunk down a little at the words and nodded, "Of course, but there are some things we need to do just in case-"

"Perfect, then we'll follow behind you, might help to speed those things up," Mr. Smithson smiled, but it didn't meet his eyes.

I didn't hear the rest, either that or I didn't understand it.

All I could focus on was Mara, and how she was in her worst nightmare. I might have had triggers, but she had more. Small spaces were always her worst. She probably looked like a mad woman in the cell.

Someone nudged me. Snapping me out of my thoughts. James was looking at me, concerned in his eyes.

"She's going to be fine, we're just going to get her, get out, and come back here. Simple."

I nodded, though part of me didn't want to go back once we got Mara. James and I were talking. And if we got her, and came back here, I felt that would end again, because we'd be back in reality.

And I didn't want something that felt so good to end.

Us talking, that felt right.

Heavy breathing. Back up against the tree.

Wrong.

I needed Mara. I needed to talk to her.

She'd know what to do. At least, I hoped she did.

James and I made our way to the back of the wagon, my heart racing.

Mara didn't do well in confined spaces. She didn't do well with a gun to her head.

And if she was in that confined space without anyone or anything, she was going to be in a world of trouble.

Il poliziotto found her with the gun on her after so many days without it, which meant she had a reason to need it again.

James sat next to me instead of across from me like he normally did. It was silent in the back, though a few minutes into the ride, I felt a warm hand come around my own, gripping it tight.

I jumped a little at the contact and tried to pull away. I tried to wrench my hand away from his, ignoring how comforting it was, but James held on, his ocean eyes snapping to mine.

I found myself drowning again. Not just in his eyes, but in how close he was to me. In the way his fingers intertwined with mine. In the way his palms weren't calloused like mine, but they were getting there, his skin rough, not calloused but cut up. My heart beat a little faster at how his eyes flickered between my own hazel ones, and my lips.

I should have looked away to stop the feeling bubbling up in the pit of my stomach, the little flip flops it was doing. But I never did.

"Everythings gonna be okay, Luca," he said softly, his thumb rubbing the top of my hand.

And for some reason, I trusted his words, that everything was going to be okay, even if it wasn't right now.

Hold on just a little longer, Mara, just a little longer.

Mara

The cell was cold. They didn't give me a blanket, or anything else for that matter and I found myself crouched in the corner closest to the door where I knew there would be some warmth. I wasn't as worried about being cold, as I was about how I didn't have a gun on me. I didn't have something to keep me safe.

My mind raced, switching from my gun, to Marco, to the walls closing in around me. I shivered. I couldn't tell if it was the cold, or the image of Marco's dead body flashing in my mind. I wondered how many shots were fired, how many seconds he'd been alive after the hot lead cut through him.

It took two bullets for me to bring down my first. Then I learned to shoot at the head, not the chest.

My image of Marco changed from two to the heart, to one in the brain, blood dripping down into his open eyes.

I'd seen that happen before. I hadn't bothered closing

the ENR soldiers' eyes. They could die with blood in their eyes. Now, I really hoped someone had closed Marco's eyes, so he couldn't see his own blood.

My mind flipped over to the supply runs and ambushes we'd run. The gunshots. The blood. It had gotten on my boots. The ones I was wearing right now actually. My eyes shifted over to them. I could still see spots on them. Splatter marks on the toes. It was more than just Amelia's blood on them.

The last time we ambushed a supply crate. I didn't even blink.

My heart sped up with the image of another lifeless body. And then another, and another. Blood on my hands. Blood on my face. Another memory surfaced.

I had been running from a soldier during an ambush, it had been a bloodbath on both sides. Back when all the resistance groups were in *Napoli* trying to plan where they would go from there. We'd been taking advantage of the numbers.

There had been heavy gunfire. Blood flowed into the streets, and pooled in the cracks of the cobblestone. I was running, we were falling back, trying to get an advantage in the alleys. I'd tripped over something, and fell down. A bullet found its way to me while I was on the ground. It was a surface wound, barely grazing me. My leg burned as if I was witnessing it all over again, and I could hear the gunshots now, smell the scent of blood.

The memory kept going. My hands had reached out to break my fall and landed in something sticky and warm, and when my palms slipped, my face dove right into it. It got in my mouth, and I tasted the distinctly metallic liquid.

It was blood.

I had fallen into a pool of blood. The face of a dead ENR soldier centimeters from mine. I stared into his eyes. Dark brown. Cloudy. Lifeless.

I wasn't in the cell in Falmouth anymore, I'd tried to hold onto reality as much as I could, but I couldn't. My mind put me on the cool cobblestone, covered in blood. Staring into those eyes.

My hands shook.

I was rocking back and forth on my heels.

I was having an attack.

In a jail cell where I knew I was being watched.

I probably looked like a madwoman.

But those eyes.

Dark.

Lonely.

Dead.

Just like Marcos would be.

It was too much.

I closed my eyes.

But when I did, the image of that ENR soldier's body was replaced with Marco's. I was laying in his blood, feeling it seep into my clothes, coating my hands and face.

In the distance, above the gunshots and the yelling, I heard a door open, but I was too far gone to tell if it was mine, or three cells down.

Arms came around my body.

I flinched, trying to kick whoever was trying to pull me off the ground, trying to take me away from Marco.

I could have protected him.

I could have saved him.

He hadn't been there when I had needed him, and guilt had plagued him. I had seen it in his eyes at that train station. Yet the one time he actually needed me by his side, I wasn't. He lost his life because I wasn't there.

Could someone ever forgive a person for that?

"Mara, *apri gli occhi, perfavore.*"

Mara, open your eyes.

I recognized the voice.

Luca.

My eyes fluttered open to find Luca in front of me.

"*Stai bene?*"

I started to say something, and then I thought of Marco, and *la Resistenza,* and how he'd died doing the one thing we planned to do together.

I wasn't okay.

I wasn't okay at all.

I had been broken before, shattered.

But now, I was ash.

I felt tears start to roll down my face, and as I tried to speak, my voice cracked, so I just shook my head.

"What happened? What did they do to you?"

I shook my head again, looking up at two hazel eyes I knew well, with my own which were blurry with tears.

"Marco." I was able to get out.

Luca's expression changed, as if understanding. He knew as soon as I said the name, and I felt his arms around me pulling me closer to him.

"We're gonna get you out of here."

"Who?" I squeeked.

"Mr. Smithson, James, and I."

I looked at him, shocked that they were here, "What?"

"Yeah, we're leaving." He paused for a second before he reached behind him, "I got something for you."

I watched him pull out a Beretta pistol. My gun.

I snatched it away from him and felt the worn grip fit right into my hand. I relaxed a little, letting out a breath. I could protect myself now. My racing heart started to slow down and my breathing was getting steadier by the second with the gun in my hand.

"Do you think you can get up?"

The tears streaming down my face were wiped away quickly by my hand. I wasn't going to cry again. Not here anyway. I took a shaky breath, and gathered myself, even if it felt like my composure was being held together by a single fraying thread.

I cleared my throat and rolled my eyes, "Luca, I've faced Nazis and ENR soldiers dozens of times, I am quite certain standing up won't be a problem."

He smiled. I knew the look.

She's back.

I got that look on my face when I calmed him down too.

"Okay, let's get the *fanculo* out of here."

"*Concordata.*"

Agreed.

He stood up, offering me a hand which I readily took. Once I was up, I stuffed my gun into the waistband of my pants again. I glanced at Luca, tears were starting to brim his eyes as he stared straight ahead. I knew the face, I knew the look, and I knew what he was thinking.

"He died fighting for the right side, Luca, in the end, he was one of us again."

He nodded. I knew it wouldn't make a huge difference in the grief, but I was shouldering a lot of guilt and grief. I didn't want his mind to be clouded with the same thoughts I was having.

The cold night air hit my face as Luca and I left the jail, James following close behind us. Mr. Smithson took a little longer to get out of the concrete block. He was busy yelling at the *poliziotto* for being a "bloody idiot," which I for one thought was an ingenious insult.

James was about to sit next to Luca in the carriage, but then stopped himself for some reason, choosing to sit opposite to us.

There was a silent agreement between Luca and I that we wouldn't tell anyone about Marco's passing. In this war, people were dying left and right, it wasn't a surprise anymore. Telling the Smithsons would only result in looks of pity and sympathy. We both didn't want that.

So we sat in silence on the ride home, as if what happened on the beach was all that was going on. As if someone hadn't just died.

Luca looked like he wanted to tell me something. His eyes kept shifting over to me, and his mouth would slowly start to open before clamping shut again after glancing at James. When we finally got back to the house after what seemed like hours of silence, the three of us rushed up to our rooms after Mr. Smithson said we should all get some sleep. It had been a long night, and I sure as hell intended to shut the door to my room and never come out.

I let out a breath as I crossed the threshold, finding some sort of safety being back in the room. The creaking of the floorboards behind me made me turn around just in time to see Luca barge into the room, shutting the door behind him.

I stood there as he paced the room. Back and forth and back and forth, over and over until I was certain he was going to make me sick.

I raised my eyebrow.

This was what always happened when he wanted to

tell me something.

He'd pace until he exploded.

And based on previous experiences that was going to be in five, four, three, two-

"I kissed James."

Merda.

I looked at him.

I blinked.

I blinked again.

He kissed James.

I should have been shocked.

I should have been appalled like his *nonna* would have been.

I should have thrown a Bible at him.

Lucky for him, I was not a God fearing woman.

And luckily, about a week ago, I had broken a sacred 'rule' myself thanks to Will, and I hated hypocrites.

I nodded, "Alright."

I expected him to sigh, to be happy I wasn't mad. But instead, he threw his hands up violently.

"Alright? This is not alright, Mara. This is horrible. How could you be okay with something like this?"

"Would you rather me tell you how much you've 'disappointed God and your *nonna*?'"

"Yes!"

I jumped at the volume his voice had reached. Luca never yelled. He never threw himself around. He was always calm. But now, his eyes were blazing, he looked like he was going to combust.

He was furious.

I didn't know if the anger was directed at himself, at me, or at the people in the church who'd talked about love between a man and a woman.

And saving yourself until marriage.

Anddd… Moving on.

"Okay, Luca, you need to calm down."

"Calm down? Mara, I kissed James."

"And?"

"He. Is. A. Boy."

I nodded, "Yes, Luca, he is. And you kissed him."

I crossed the room to him, putting my hands on his shoulders, slowly guiding him towards my bed so he could sit down. The pacing was getting to be too much, a few more laps around my room and I was going to need a bucket. We both sat on the bed, letting it dip under our weight.

Luca looked at me, "But it was wrong."

I blinked, "Why, Luca? Why is kissing him so wrong?"

"Because, Mara, God said-"

"The Bible said. Luca, that tattered old book was written by men who didn't know what they were talking about. Okay? Do you like him?"

Luca looked at the ground, "I don't think-"

"Do you like him?"

He let out a breath, "Yes," he whispered, almost as if he said it any louder, it would make it real.

"What did it feel like when you kissed him?"

A pause, "Like my whole body was going to catch fire."

"Did it feel right?"

"Yes, it did, but the Bible-"

I scoffed, standing up, "*Fanculo la Bibbia*, Luca. Alright? You're really going to let an old book tell you what to do? We could die in a year, a month, maybe even a week. Life right now is so unpredictable, Luca, we don't have enough certainty to be held accountable for following the rules of a God that abandoned the world in its darkest hour. We don't have the time to worry about *L'uomo nero* coming if we break the rules. So for fucks sake, Luca, break one damn rule so you can be happy. If James makes you feel happy, if you like him, then do something about it."

He sat in silence, before looking at me, standing up, "I can't believe I'm saying this, but, you're right, Mara."

"Am I?"

"Yes. After what happened to Marco, I mean, that could have been any of us."

I nodded sadly, shifting my eyes downward, "Yeah. It could've."

I felt his arms come around me in a hug, warming me up.

"But it wasn't," Luca said.

I buried my head into his chest, "And yet why does it feel like it was?"

"Grief is powerful, Mara. We all know it," his voice shook at the end.

I nodded, and didn't talk for a moment, because I knew we both needed some sort of reassurance we were alright.

"Thank you for not throwing a Bible at me," Luca muttered under his breath.

I laughed quietly, the rise and fall of my chest matching his. He was laughing too.

"Where the hell would I get one of those things?"

"I don't know, there might be a few spares around the house."

I smiled. Knowing Mrs. Smithson, there probably were. Luca let go of me, stepping towards the door, but he turned right as he was crossing the threshold.

"Mara?"

"Hm?"

"Why *are* you so calm about this?"

I smiled to myself, "Because I'm not really one to judge you about breaking the rules."

He returned the smile, thinking it was for him, "Well, thank you," he said as he left.

Wait for it...

Three, two-

Luca almost threw himself into my room, "What the hell did you do?"

CHAPTER 18

**October 29th, 1943, 7:23am, Falmouth,
Cornwall, England
Luca**

I was crazy.

I was insane.

It was a bad idea.

It was a *really* bad idea.

But there I was, pretending to be asleep, trying to coax myself out of bed so I could do something horribly stupid because I might die today.

I needed him to wake up.

And when he did, I was going to tell him, I was going to kiss him, and everything was going to be okay.

Except for the hundreds of things that could go wrong.

What if he thought the kiss was a mistake?

What if I forgot what I'd been rehearsing to say all night?

What if a bomb went off in this house, and blew us to bits before I could even say anything?

I let out a breath.

I was being pathetic.

My eyes shot open, tired of trying to prepare myself for failure. If I didn't do it, Mara would've probably held her gun to my head and forced me to.

I rolled over, facing James's bed. He wasn't there, which

was either an act of *Dio,* or the worst case scenario. I shot up from the mattress, maybe he was changing or something in the bathroom. We'd both started doing that in the past two weeks, changing in the same room had gotten uncomfortable. I was going to wait a minute, but I saw a sheet of paper on my nightstand, neat yet shaky handwriting in English.

Went for a walk on beach

~ James

I let out a breath. I needed to tell him. I felt like I was going to throw up. Bees kept bringing their stingers to the lining of my stomach.

And it hurt.

I was still wearing the clothes I had on from the day before, but I'd taken off my button up in the night, I'd gotten too hot with it on. So now I was in just my tweed pants and a white undershirt tucked into them.

I hopped back and forth around the room trying to put my shoes on, hoping they were already tied. Trying to not spend any more time in the space James and I shared. I knew if I stayed in the room any longer, I'd find a way to talk myself out of the terrible idea I'd thought of.

I went down the stairs as quietly as I could so I didn't wake up Mara, who was probably still in her room, or get the attention of Mr. and Mrs. Smithson. Once I cleared the stairs, I raced out of the house. I'd never been on the beach before, but I'd watched from my window as Mara would go down to stare at the ocean. I bounded down the steps, missing one, regaining my balance, and kept going down. My heart was beating so fast I was afraid that it would leap out of my chest. Then I'd be dead. Maybe that was better than what I was planning to do.

This was a horrible idea.

Too soon, my feet sank into the dry sand, and the feeling of wanting to throw up grew in my stomach.

I was already halfway there. I couldn't turn around.

Or you could.

Mara wouldn't turn around.

No, she'd walk right up to James and tell him.

She wouldn't hesitate.

Well, maybe it was time to be like my best friend for once.

My eyes shifted to the right, searching for James, and all too soon my eyes found a mop of blonde hair. He stood close to the water, letting it wash over his shoes. His gaze was trained on the open ocean and his hair blew in the wind. He hadn't put pomade in it, probably too early for that anyway.

I started walking towards him, even if I wanted to turn around, my body wouldn't let me. My mind was a jumbled mess as I tried to remember what I was going to say when I got to him.

James, I'm sorry for not talking to you, but I was scared. I was scared of my thoughts, and of how I felt. And us kissing, didn't help me get away from my feelings. What I'm trying to say is, you make me happy. Talking to you makes me happy. Your eyes make me happy. That kiss, that made me happy. Please, please, please, don't be upset. And if the whole thing was a mistake, then, uh, forget we had this conversation.

Or something like that.

I'd been rehearsing since I had got in bed the night before, but I still wasn't satisfied with what I wanted to say. There was so much I needed to tell him. But I either couldn't translate it, or couldn't figure out how to put the way he made me feel into words.

Maybe it was for the best.

I was getting closer and the sound of the waves overlapped the sound of my feet struggling against the sand. In that moment, two blue eyes turned to lock with mine.

James had seen me.

He gave me a small smile, "Hey, Luca."

My mind went blank. I forgot what I was going to say, all the words had escaped, leaving my mouth dry. I was stuck looking into his eyes, and they were drowning me, down, down, down, into their depths. My heart picked up speed, and all I could think about was what Mara had said earlier.

Fanculo la Bibbia.

"Luca?"

I blinked.

I took more steps towards him and when I got close to him, I couldn't help my hazel eyes drifting towards his lips. The lips I'd kissed two weeks ago, and loved every second of it. His eyes were doing the same, but he looked confused, my silence wasn't helping.

"Luca, are you-"

I took a deep breath, *"Fanculo la Bibbia."*

My hand went to cup his cheek, like he had done to mine the last time, pulling him closer to me. I paused for a second, centimeters away from his lips, trying to get a grip on what exactly I was about to do. But in that moment, I stopped trying to think it through, and instead, crashed my lips against his.

Every inch of my body felt like it was going to explode as I held him tighter and his hands came around my waist. Everywhere he touched sent a burning sensation through me, scorching every part of me.

I didn't want to stop.

I wanted to stay like this.

This was better than anything I'd ever felt before. Us. This felt right. If a bomb hit the beach at this moment, I would die happy. I'd be happy because I did this.

And just as quick as it had all started, right as my fear was fading, it felt like James was pulling away. His hands stayed on my waist, but even then, his eyes, the two blue oceans, looked scared.

"Luca, we, we can't."

But his arms were holding me so tight, I knew he didn't want that to be true. So I connected our lips again, hoping he knew we could. And we were.

He pulled away again, "But, what if-?"

I knew what he was thinking. I was thinking about it too, but I didn't want to think, so I kissed him again.

"Luca-"

Kiss.

"The consequences-"

Kiss.

He pulled away for the third time, but I was the one talking, "Later."

"But-"

I huffed a little, "James, I am trying to kiss you right now, so could you please *chiudi quella cazzo di bocca?*"

He gave me a small smile, "I don't even know what that means."

"It means shut up," I said before catching his lips with mine.

I knew we needed to talk about it. I knew there would be consequences to whatever came out of this kiss. But right now, I didn't want to focus on that. We could worry about everything later. I was kissing James, and that was all that mattered in the world at this moment.

And in a world filled with uncertainty, I didn't have

time to follow rules laid out by people who lived centuries before me.

Right now, I needed to be happy. And I was.

And that was how it was going to stay.

October 31st, 1943, 6:29pm, Falmouth, Cornwall, England
Mara

I had stayed in my room most of the day. I didn't want to come out. It had been a couple of days since I was in the cramped prison cell, and I still didn't want to leave my room. Luca had been bringing up bits of food to give to me, and dropping off books he got from James. According to him, things were good. He hadn't really told me a lot other than that, but last time he said anything, he'd told me they were talking about how the hell they were going to keep what they were doing a secret.

I was perfectly content to stay in my room for as long as I could. Getting out would make everything real. I'd have to face Mr. Smithson, who most definitely had told Mrs. Smithson. I could picture the lecture now of how I shouldn't carry a gun. It wasn't safe for a woman to carry a weapon.

But it wasn't safe to not carry one either.

I'd have to face the real world. I'd have to try to ignore the fact that I'd been arrested.

It disgusted me. Not how I got arrested, but how the officer thought I ran in the same group as Mussolini. I never wanted to be associated with that *bastardo* ever again.

I hadn't been sleeping either. I was too scared about the nightmares I knew I would have. I'd had so many flashbacks I was terrified of what I would see in my sleep. And when I did surrender to exhaustion once or twice, I'd wake up in a cold sweat shortly thereafter. My gun wasn't under my pillow anymore either. I held it in my hand every night, a voice in the back of my head telling me I was next, and then Luca.

I wanted to run away to a place where no one would ever find me.

I wanted to fade away from people's minds.

At one point I even considered joining Marco in his eternal sleep, because at least then I'd be at peace.

I was messed up beyond repair.

I knew my mind would never be the same after this war. The nightmares would never go away. The flashbacks, the panic attacks, they'd never go away. They'd always be there. A reminder of what I'd done, and who I'd hurt. What I'd lost.

Who I'd lost.

I thought of Will, and how he'd never harmed anyone in this war. He spent his days stitching other people up.

There wasn't enough thread in the world to stitch my mind back together.

I'd been avoiding him. Not leaving the room also meant I wasn't meeting him in the field, or on the beach, and when the sun went down, and I knew he was standing outside my window, waiting for me to come down, I stayed in bed.

Plink.

What the-

Plink.

Plink.

I sat up from my bed, wondering where the noise was coming from, the gun clenched tightly in my hand, preparing myself for the worst.

Plink.

My head whipped over to the window. I stared at it for a second before a pebble flew up and hit the glass.

Plink.

I went to the window, gun pointed but hidden on my torso.

Merda.

I put the gun in my waistband, tucking my shirt over it so it wasn't visible.

I couldn't pretend I hadn't seen him, but I didn't feel like going for a walk, and I certainly didn't feel like acting as if nothing was wrong with me.

But, perhaps, just maybe, this was the day that I needed to stop pretending.

I opened the window and looked down at where I saw dark hair and blue eyes gazing up at me. The sun was setting and it cast a golden glow around Will, making him look even more charming as he smiled up at me.

"'Ello, Mara. 'Ow was your jailbreak?"

I let out a breath, "You heard?"

"The 'ole town did, most excitin' thing to 'appen to this place since the port got bombed. Falmouth's very own Italian spy. If you ask me, it's all very dramatic," he said with a smirk playing on his lips.

"Oh?"

"Yeah. I mean, you're not quite the best spy in the world."

"And why's that?" I asked, playing along with this game.

"Because, your British accent is 'orrible."

My mouth dropped, "Is not."

"Definitely is."

I rolled my eyes, "Whatever."

Will motioned for me to come down, "Come on, Juliet, climb down the tower for your Romeo."

I couldn't help laugh a little. I needed to get out of the house. I needed to get out of my room, the isolation had been killing me, but I hadn't wanted to leave. Avoiding the truth made the pain go away easier. It always did.

But I couldn't help feeling like I needed to tell Will about everything.

About me.

How I wasn't strong and brave.

I was broken and weak.

How I had been shattered into pieces so many times that I'd forgotten how to put myself back together the way I was before the war.

I took a deep breath before nodding to him. I climbed down, gripping the dying ivy for support. In a few days there wouldn't be much left to hold onto. I might've actually had to walk out the front door.

Once my feet hit the ground, I looked at Will, "Don't they both die in the end?"

Will paused for a minute, thinking about this idea.

"Yeah, yeah they do. But, they live out an epic love story."

"After three days of knowing each other."

I was able to get my hands on the book back in school when I was younger, I used to think it was the best romance in the entire world. Now I just focused on how even after trying so hard to be together, they had to die for it to happen.

In the back of my mind, I knew the same thing was probably true for me and Will. Because deep down, I knew whatever we had wouldn't last. After the war, who knew what would happen. I didn't even know if we'd live to see the end of it.

We walked down to the beach in a comfortable silence, our shoulders bumping every once and a while. I honestly was just glad he was with me. He felt normal. He wasn't tied to *Italia* or the things I did there, and he didn't make me think of all the things that could go wrong in my uncertain life.

I thought we were going to walk a little more in silence once we reached the ocean, but that wasn't the case.

"Why 'ave you been avoidin' me?"

Fanculo.

"I'm not avoiding you."

"Really? So for the past few days you've been stayin' away from your window, if you've left the 'ouse you've been avoidin' the field, and you 'aven't been on the beach. If that isn't avoidin' me then I don't know what the bloody 'ell is."

No way out.

I had to tell him.

I really liked him. But I needed to tell him. It was better if he knew.

I let out a breath, "Yeah. You're right."

"Why are you?"

Another breath.

"Because, I finally figured out I can't be a part of *this*," I motioned in between us.

"Mara-"

I knew he was going to try to talk me out of what I was saying. And if I let him speak, he would. I knew he would, because of the way he was looking at me. The way his eyes said he more than just liked me. It was the way Marco had once looked at me. And Will's eyes alone were enough to make me stop talking and just ignore everything. But I had already started. I couldn't stop. He needed to know.

"Will, my head is messed up. This war, the things I've done, they've all just scrambled my mind up. I can't sleep because I'll have nightmares. I can't leave my room because I'm afraid something will set me off and I'll have a flashback of someone I've killed, or I'll start having an attack."

I pulled out my gun, "I sleep with this gun in my hand, and I take it everywhere because I'm afraid someone's going to try to kill me and I won't have anything to protect myself and the people I care about." I paused to catch my breath, "And if all that isn't enough to drive someone away, then I don't know what is."

A hand came around mine, the one with the gun in it, and I tensed. Will lifted my chin up, making me look him in the eyes, the two ice blocks that left me frozen in place.

"Mara, you couldn't drive me away even if you tried."

I blinked, "I did try, did you not just hear everything I said?"

Will smiled, "I 'eard you, Mara. And it's okay to be a little messed up after what's 'appened to you."

"Will, I am *broken*."

He got closer to me, eyes never leaving my own, "Mara, I'm not gonna get driven away because you say you're broken. I'm a doctor. I put people back together."

"You can't put me back together, Will, my mind is too far gone."

"Then I'll 'old you when you 'ave an attack. I'll stay the night, so when you 'ave a nightmare I'm there to wake you up and 'old you tight enough for you to know you're safe. I'll make sure you never leave the 'ouse without your gun. You might be broken, Mara, but the pieces still make up the 'ole, and I fell for the 'ole. Everythin' about you Mara. So, I'll be by your side even when your broken pieces are showin'."

I blinked, "Will, when the war's over, *if* it ever is over, I might never see you again, you do realize that right?"

"Why?"

"I belong in *Italia*, fighting for freedom I've never felt before."

"But what if there's nothin' to fight for? What if Italy's alright? What if it doesn't need people fightin' for it anymore?"

I never had thought about that. I'd always accepted the reality that I might not live to see my country's freedom. I'd never gone beyond war.

"I don't know what I'll do."

Will held my hands in his, a soft breeze blew across the sand, "Then stay 'ere, or go to London. There'll be jobs to 'elp restore the parts of the city that 'ave been blown to bits, and there'll likely be relief groups seekin' 'elp. You don't 'ave to be fightin' to 'elp a country recover."

It sounded like a great idea. No more fighting. No more running. I'd be helping, without hurting anyone, I'd be supporting a cause without having to fight for it with a gun.

I'd be safe.

But still, I hesitated.

What was my life without fighting for the freedom I'd always wanted?

It was at that moment I realized the freedom I'd felt in Falmouth, in *Inghilterra*, was more freedom than I'd ever received in my life. *Italia* was on its way to independence. The Allies were invading, civil war was breaking out with support from the West. We could be free before the war ended. I wanted to fight. I wanted to stand up for freedom. But I didn't want to hurt any more people. I didn't want my nightmares to be fueled by more bodies.

I had helped start the revolution.

Perhaps it wasn't my job to finish it.

I looked at Will, who was gazing down at me with such intensity, it felt like it was burning my entire existence.

"Stay here. With me."

"Will…" I drew out.

"Stay."

One word, four letters. A word that didn't exactly catch me off guard, but seemed to hit me as if I had just been shot.

A word that reconfigured my plans for the future, and I couldn't help myself from smiling at that future.

I nodded, "I think that sounds like a brilliant idea."

His eyes lit up, his hands left my own, and instead gripped the sides of my waist. When his hold on me tightened, I felt my feet clinging to air. He picked me up and spun me around in circles. We were laughing, and when he brought me down, he held me close in his arms.

My smile never went away. For the first time, I could imagine a future after the war. In a free country, with Will, and Luca, who'd told me that he was staying here after it ended. When I asked why, he said he couldn't go back to the place that caused him so much pain. I understood what he meant. The war had taken everything from me. It took my family, it took my life, it took my mind, it took away my hope. And yet, on the beach that evening, I felt that hope return. I felt like I had a chance.

I felt safe.

For the first time since the war began, I had my hope back.

Hope that the war would end soon. Hope that the Allies would win. Hope that Will was right. That my broken pieces put together made a whole, and that I would be alright.

In Will's arms, with the hope of a future of freedom, I knew then, I would be alright.

Everything was going to be fine.

I was going to be okay.

It would take me a while, but I would get there.

I'd be okay.

Will would be okay.

Luca would be okay.

James would be okay.

We were all going to be okay.

EPILOGUE

May 8th, 1945, 3:14pm, London, England, V-E Day
Mara

Music filled my ears as people danced in the streets, laughing, crying, yelling.

It was beautiful.

I looked behind me at Luca, who was staring with the same amazement at what would hopefully go down in history as the biggest celebration of the century. James was right beside him, their hands interwoven between their bodies, so close together I could barely see the connection.

I couldn't help but smile, they were hiding it well from everyone, but I knew what had happened. Luca couldn't keep his mouth shut once they got over the whole, I fancy a boy, thing. It was all, James this, and James that, and did I know that he wants to go into education and be a teacher? Eventually I was going to have to tell him to shut the *fanculo* up.

Though, I wasn't exactly one to talk. I snuck a glance at the boy keeping his arm around my shoulders. His icy eyes drifted towards me, and he smiled, leaning down to touch our foreheads together.

"You doin' alright?"

I couldn't say anything, I didn't know what to say, it was all so overwhelming. So I just nodded.

I never thought this would happen.

That the fighting would be over.

But it was.

"Beautiful, ain't it?" he whispered in my ear.

Another nod.

England's blue, white, and red flag hung off balconies, and people were throwing confetti, or at least pieces of paper that were torn up. They held up the newspapers. *Victory! Germany Quits! V-E Day! It's all over!*

It was all over.

It was finally all over.

All that fighting.

All that killing.

And now, it was all done with.

I wanted to cry. I wanted to scream. I wanted to shoot at something. I wanted to punch something. I wanted to grab Mussolini's cold dead body and yell at the top of my lungs, 'You see that? We did it. We beat you. You were nothing. Rot and burn in hell you son of a bitch!'

But before I could find a way to get to Italy and bring the dead former dictator back to life for one last beating, James's voice coaxed me out of my thoughts.

"I see them."

I looked at him, a letter clutched in his hand. A message from his parents. The contents told him where they'd be today in London, seeing as it was finally safe to go back. The letter had come late the night before, the day the papers declared Germany had surrendered. Then came the politics, the signing, and now we were here, and James had found his parents in a giant crowd of people.

Supposedly there was a coffee shop the family used to visit frequently before the war, and that was the place they were going to meet. We'd been waiting outside for an hour, and that whole time I couldn't help worrying that maybe, just maybe, they weren't going to come.

James had his suitcase packed and everything. Ready to go home. In fact, all four of us, him, Luca, Will, and I had luggage. We were eighteen, and now the war was over, it marked the start of us trying to get normal lives. Luca had been selling drawings back in Falmouth and planned to do the same thing here. He'd saved up a good bit of money too. He was going to stay close to James though, only a few minutes away in an apartment building. I smiled a little as I watched James grip his hand tighter and drag him over to an older couple. Both with blonde hair.

I could see where he got it from.

Will and I followed closely behind. And I felt a warm feeling in my stomach as I watched James wrap his parents in a giant hug. Though, he never let go of Luca's hand, even if Luca wanted him to. I chuckled a little at Luca's alarmed face. He'd tried to pull back, but James just gripped his hand tighter.

I glanced at Will.

We had our own plans. A friend of his grandfather was taking him under his wing at a private practice there in London. Will supposedly was going to be needed with all the soldiers coming back from war not being able to afford medical care. I guess having experience with a girl who struggled with shell-shock was going to come in handy with all those men and women coming back with horror stories. And while he was stitching people up, I was going to help with a relief group.

But all that could wait.

Right now, I was focused on the scene unfolding before me and the happiness in James's eyes when he pulled away from his parents.

"I missed you two," he said, voice cracking.

His mother was crying, her bright blue eyes sparkling in the sun.

Now I was really starting to notice the resemblance.

"We missed you as well, James," she said.

She then noticed Luca standing there, and then she shifted her eyes over to me and Will who were standing only a few steps away from the reunion.

"And who might you three be?"

"This is Luca," James said, almost too quickly, like he had been waiting to say it since the minute he saw them.

His mother smiled, "Lovely to meet you Luca. We're James's parents."

Luca nodded, "Nice to meet you both."

His accent still hadn't gone away in the year and a half we'd been in England, but his English was almost completely fluent. There were just a few words he still didn't understand.

He was like a ten-year-old learning a new word everyday.

He shook James's father's hand without hesitating. However, I could see the fear in his eyes as he stared at the father of the person he loved.

"And who might you two be?"

I smiled, "Mara."

James's mother blinked, "Mara, where are you and Luca from? You both have accents and your names are so, well, foreign."

Luca grew tense, but I straightened a little. I stuffed a hand into my skirt pocket to hold my papers while I said it.

"I'm an English citizen, Miss."

"No, but where are you *from*?"

Will looked at me for a second, arm still wrapped around my shoulder, and he pulled me closer to him as if to offer extra protection from the inquisitive eyes of James's mother.

I just smiled, pulling out the pieces of paper.

My identification.

My passport.

My citizenship.

"Says here I'm a citizen of England, Miss. I think that's what's important."

Her gaze turned understanding. It must have added up. The accent, the names, the papers. We weren't from here. But we lived here now.

She turned to James and pointed at me, "Is she single?"

Will cleared his throat, and she blinked, "Oh. Pardon me..." James's mother drifted off, not knowing what to refer to the boy so close beside me.

"Will," he said to clarify.

"Will, terribly sorry," turning her attention back towards James, she spoke again, "Apparently you missed your opportunity with this one."

When she turned to talk to Luca about something like the weather, or how he liked London, or how he and her son met, James looked back at me and offered a wink. I smirked a little and shrugged before slowly stepping back along with Will, away from the two lovebirds and James's unknowing parents.

We were going to meet back with Mr. Smithson when Big Ben struck five. He had so graciously offered to take us to London early in the morning in his car, which he hadn't taken out since the war started. I couldn't wait to hear what Luca would tell me about how terrified he was of James's father, who probably wouldn't speak much the entire time.

The music and voices overwhelmed me once again as Will and I were pulled into the crowd of happy people. And I couldn't help being happy with them. Cars drove by with people in them, soldiers waving large British flags, small infantries coming home to their families, driving around and waving to all of us. Waving to the people who'd never seen what they'd seen, to the people who wouldn't understand.

I understood, and offered a small nod to the man in the back of one of those cars who'd stopped smiling and waving. Instead, just sitting there on the verge of tears.

It didn't take me long to shift my attention over to the police cars zipping through the streets, sirens blaring, British flags attached to the backs, and soldiers with trumpets and wind instruments marching through the streets, playing a song that sounded patriotic.

All of this. It was incredible.

It was peace.

It was something I'd never seen in my life before, and that brought tears to my eyes.

"Will?"

He glanced over at me, a tear running down my cheek, and he instantly took his arm off my shoulder, and pulled me into a hug.

"Yeah, Mara?"

"Is this what freedom looks like?"

I could feel him smiling against my face.

"Yes. This is what freedom looks like."

I tried to hold back the tears, the ones blurring my vision.

Freedom.

With that word, I couldn't stop the drops of water trickling down my face.

No dictator telling us what we should think, no raids that take away family, no fighting people from the same country because one side wanted democracy and the other side wanted complete control.

Freedom.

Finally.

Will pulled away after I'd stopped crying, but he still held me close. I watched as he grabbed a small flag from an old man passing by holding handfuls of them, giving them away to anyone who wanted one. He waved it high in the air, cheering as another group of soldiers passed. I couldn't stop myself from trying to cheer louder. We went back and forth in our yelling, until the people around us moved away thinking we were insane. He smiled at me, getting a glint of something in his eye, the look he got when he was going to do something rash and unwarranted.

His arm flew to my waist, gripped me tight, and I felt myself being lowered. Dipped.

He was dipping me.

I blinked. Will was just centimeters away from me, our noses brushing together. My heart started racing like it always did when he was this close.

"We won, Mara."

"We won," I repeated, the realization washing over me.

He pulled me into him, holding me so tight I felt like I couldn't breathe. His lips pressed against mine in a way he'd only ever done once or twice before. This was a kiss that had every emotion in it. Love, happiness, joy. The feeling that finally, *finally,* the nightmare had ended. It was a good morning kiss. We had finally woken up from the terrible dream that had plagued the last five years.

We were no longer fleeing.

We were at peace.

There would always be times when the good guys didn't win.

But this was not one of those times.

AUTHORS NOTES

Oh my *fottuto dio* I made it. It took a second to get here, and a lot of frustrating nights, glaring at a blank page wondering how I was going to finish this book. And then there were of course my favorite bursts of creativity at two in the morning, leaving me an exhausted wreck. But, despite a lot of what my friends said, the sleep deprivation was worth it.

The journey to get here was, in all actuality, a few years worth of work. Not exactly on this specific book, but on my writing journey in general.

This book started out as a class assignment in Health class, and now, well, it's become *this.* This book was the product of many midnight writing sessions and a lot of chocolate and hot cocoa, and I'm very happy to say I now have a book to show for it. I always wanted to say I'd published a book, instead of just saying I'm in the process of writing one. I think that might just be the fact that writers are never quite taken seriously until we have a hard copy in our hand. But now, I have the hard copy to show for all those late nights and intricate whiteboard storyboarding. The journey to get here was long and difficult. My first book I ever decided to put out into the world got rejected from many literary agents, and I learned very quickly how to get a no, and then I learned that it's okay to let go of an idea that isn't working. That book is a part of my writing journey as much as this one is, because it's always the things that you mess up that lead you to the thing you got right.

This book, to me, was probably my first real success. Not that there were other times where I felt successful as a writer, but this was the first book I felt incredibly comfortable putting out into the world for everyone to see, and not only that, I would feel proud to call it my book.

I think I developed a love for historical fiction as soon as I started reading books like Refugee, Making Bombs for Hitler, and Wait For Me. Specifically, I fell in love with World War II novels. So it made a lot of sense when I started getting into writing within the genre, and this book is just a show of how much love I have for historical fiction. I enjoyed researching the Italian Resistance and the dates corresponding with it. I think at the start of the book when I was deciding on the years and months I got really scared of how I was going to make everything line up. Luckily for me, a lot of stuff happened in September. I really loved looking into outfits and clothing that each character would wear, and exploring what kind of guns the Italian army used before Mussolini came to power. It was just those details that I loved putting into the book.

Apart from the research, I had so much fun writing the character interactions, and working out the character growth in this book, especially for Mara, who I got to play around with a lot.

Mara was the incredibly strong and resilient female protagonist I felt needed to be written about. A girl who didn't let the gender norms of the time hold her back and who didn't let tradition stand in the way. Not only this, but someone who'd overcome great trials, only to come out the other side stronger, even if she didn't realize it yet.

Mara's belief in justice and freedom pushed her to become the woman she was. Beliefs I believe we need to keep alive today.

Though romance is at the forefront of this novel, behind all of that lies a message of hope for the future, hope for freedom, and the ability to fight for what is right. Things we need to remember to believe in in this world.

This book has been an incredible journey, and one that is only the start of a much larger one that I hope will continue for a very long time, a career even. And I can't wait to see where this journey takes me next.

ACKNOWLEDGE-MENTS

Thank you so much to my amazing and supportive parents, especially my mom, who was my editor on this book, and a damn good one at that. She was the one who always supported my dreams and my ideas, and the person who took me to my first writing workshop, and bought me my first and second whiteboard, and all those notebooks.

Thank you to my best friend Breanne, my partner in crime with most everything, and the best writing friend ever. She's supported me and cheered me on throughout my journey, and has had hope in my books at times when I didn't. She's helped me celebrate all my small successes. The amount of times we've both ranted to each other about our endless amounts of book ideas are endless.

And thank you to the other people who've supported me along the way, volentarily given their time to edit a chapter or two, and given me words of encouragement and excitement! And to the few people who looked down on me for my hopefulness, part of me did this out of spite.